Now You're In Trouble, Here Comes My Solicitor!

Now You're In Trouble, Here Comes My Solicitor!

Steven D Coles

Matador
9 Priory Business Park,
Wistow Road, Kibworth Beauchamp,
Leicestershire. LE8 0RX
Tel: 0116 279 2299
Email: books@troubador.co.uk
Web: www.troubador.co.uk/matador
Twitter: @matadorbooks

ISBN 978 1 8004 6401 8

British Library Cataloguing in Publication Data.
A catalogue record for this book is available from the British Library.

Printed and bound in Great Britain by 4edge Limited
Typeset in 11pt Minion Pro by Troubador Publishing Ltd, Leicester, UK

Matador is an imprint of Troubador Publishing Ltd

To Helen (Nell)
My best friend.

Contents

Part One

The tales told to provincial lawyers by their clients are many and varied. Few, however, were so perfectly bizarre as that related to recently qualified solicitor Francis Gilbert in his high street office in Plymouth by two refined old ladies one mid-December morning.

A young female head appeared around the door. "Miss Clarke and Mrs Wentworth-Jones are here, Mr Gilbert."

"That's good, Debs – they are early. Send them through."

Francis made a few desultory efforts to tidy the perennial mess on his desk and then hastened to reception to greet his clients.

"Miss Clarke, Miss Wentworth-Jones, very nice to meet you. Come through, ladies, and take a seat."

"Thank you, Mr Gilbert, and thank you for fitting us in before Christmas. We do so hope you can help us."

Both women accepted his proffered hand with elegant "Hinge-and-Bracket-esque" gestures and followed him into the ground-floor office. The room looked out onto a busy Victorian

1

thoroughfare, lined on the far side by the local Minster church, and leading past the hostelry favoured by local professionals (including Francis) to the city magistrates' court.

Francis gazed across the desk between the piles of files at his new clients. He had picked up at once the fact that their accents were not local – precise, cultured, the diction of the 1950s BBC, and yet he sensed a nervousness bordering on desperation. Knowing and understanding your client was crucial.

"Well, ladies, I suggest you tell me your story in your own words and I will ask questions as we go along. But first, could you please tell me your full names and – if I can be very presumptuous – your ages?"

"Letitia Clarke, aged seventy-seven, and this is my sister Cora Wentworth-Jones. I am the elder by two years. Shall I tell Mr Gilbert, Cora, or do you want to?"

"Oh, you do it, my dear. You are much better at keeping to the point than I am. You know how I wander."

Here, Francis exhaled an almost audible sigh of relief. The bane of the lives of busy professionals were those clients who began with the words "to cut a long story short" and then proceeded unashamedly to extend an essentially short story interminably. This, it appeared, would not be one of those cases.

"All right, Mr Gilbert, I will begin. Cora and I are tenants of a house in Mannamead – we have lived there for years."

"How long, Miss Clarke? When did you move in?"

"What year was it, Cora?"

"It was the year my husband Reggie died," said Cora, addressing Francis directly. "1969, Reggie died suddenly and his death was a terrible shock to me. I had never lived on my own. Letitia was ever so kind – she always is – and suggested we rent somewhere together. Reggie had no life assurance and…"

Letitia put her hand on her sister's arm.

"You're wandering, Cora," she said gently.

"Yes, of course, sorry. You take over, Lettie."

"The house was advertised in the *Herald* newspaper. We looked at it and it was perfect. Our landlord was a Mr Rowe – a lovely man. He bought us a bottle of wine every Christmas and we bought him Scotch."

"Did you have a tenancy agreement?"

"No, but we do now – or at least we have a document listing the terms of our tenancy sent to us by our new landlord, Mr Hyde. And we also have a fair rent."

"When did Mr Hyde become your landlord?"

"Mr Rowe died three years ago. His widow Edith was very kind but she was older than us and didn't want the bother of letting. She offered to sell the property to us at a substantial discount, but we have very little money and no one would give us a mortgage because of our age. The house is very big and in an expensive area and even with the discount it was more than we could afford."

"So, she sold it?"

"Yes, she sold it by auction – to a Mr Hyde."

Letitia's hand crept across the table to squeeze her sister's. Francis could sense their disquiet – fear, even.

There was a brief silence. Francis held back his next question to allow them a moment of reflection.

Letitia resumed – a tremor in her voice.

"That wasn't his original name – he changed his name to Mr Hyde."

Francis was on the point of asking if his real name was Dr Jekyll but sensed this might be inappropriate.

"He is every bit as sinister as his literary namesake," said Cora, as if reading his thoughts.

Letitia nodded in agreement.

"Within a few months of his buying the house, he turned up at the front door and gave us a letter telling us our rent had been doubled. He stepped into the hall uninvited and sat in our sitting room. Cora was very brave and said he shouldn't come in unless we invited him. He said he could do what he liked as it was his house and he would leave once we had countersigned the letter to agree the rent increase."

Her voice became hesitant and tremulous again and Cora took over.

"I told him we wouldn't sign anything without advice, and he told us he didn't need our agreement to increase the rent. I thought of asking him why he had requested it then, but didn't want to annoy him unnecessarily. He is a very big, unkempt-looking man and had a look about him of barely suppressed rage. I imagine he is very much as Stevenson pictured his own Mr Hyde."

"Then he stood up very quickly and we both started. I think that was what he intended – to intimidate us. He said, 'Take your advice then but don't take long – and you'd better agree to the rent increase if you want to stay living here.' And then he was gone."

"And when he had gone, we both had a little cry, didn't we, dear?" added Letitia. Cora nodded her agreement.

Francis felt they could all do with a break at this point. He had been taking vigorous notes and his hand needed a rest.

"Would you like a cup of tea, ladies?"

"Call us Lettie and Cora, Mr Gilbert. No need to be formal, and yes, we'd love a cuppa." The slangy term seemed slightly out of place in Letitia's cut-glass accent.

"Only if you call me Frank," he replied.

"Oh, we couldn't do that, Mr Gilbert," said Cora. "You're a solicitor."

"Don't be silly, darling, this is the 1980s. If Mr Gilbert is happy for us to call him Frank then Frank it is. A very fine name – our father's name."

"Good, that's settled then." Frank summoned three mugs of tea. It occurred to him that Letitia and Cora were probably more accustomed to taking the finest Assam or Darjeeling from china tea-pots via a tea-strainer, but a high-street law firm wouldn't stretch to that and they would have to make do with tea bags.

Ten minutes later, refreshed by tea and relaxed by some congenial conversation, Letitia took up the story.

"One of the ladies at our church told us her daughter worked at the Citizen's Advice Bureau. She arranged an appointment for us. We were pleasantly surprised to discover that we could ask the rent officer to assess a fair rent, and that even though this might be a little more than we were currently paying, as Mr and Mrs Rowe had never increased our rent, it would be nothing like double. We were also advised that any increase would be phased in over a period of time. They also put our minds at rest regarding our landlord's threat to evict us. They told us that he could not do this without a court order which he would struggle to get as we were almost certainly protected tenants. They qualified this by saying that they were not experts on the question of our occupation rights and that we should take advice from a solicitor specialising in tenancy matters – so hopefully you agree with them?"

"I certainly do," said Frank. "The CAB is usually right. So you applied for a fair rent?"

"We did. The CAB helped us to fill in the forms and the rent officer assessed the rent at 15% more than we were paying – which we could easily afford.

"We were delighted to receive the notification from the rent officer, but it contained the ominous, but I suppose inevitable, notice that 'a copy of this notification has been sent to your landlord'. We waited with bated breath for his reaction. Every knock on our front door would send us scurrying for the curtains. We would only answer when we were sure it was not him. But he never called. What we did receive was a letter from him a week or so later, riddled with spelling mistakes and grammatical errors, telling us that he was giving us notice to quit the house within fourteen days and that he would be turning up on the fifteenth day to change the locks.

"Off we hurried again to the CAB. They told us that the notice to quit was completely invalid. It was not in the correct form, did not contain the prescribed information and gave insufficient notice. They advised us to ignore it."

Cora now took over. "But we couldn't just do nothing and spend the next fourteen days terrified that he would turn up and throw us out on the fifteenth. So we asked the CAB to write to him for us. This they did, and told him that he could not evict us without a valid notice to quit and a court order."

"Do you have a copy of the letter?"

Letitia produced it and Frank briefly glanced through it. It was as he would have drafted it himself, except that it omitted the advice he would have given to the landlord to take the advice of his own solicitor. Often the only way to elicit a rational response from a person, without the benefit of legal advice intent on riding roughshod over the rights of others, was for that person to receive confirmation of those rights from his or her own solicitor.

"We heard nothing for several weeks – and began to hope that Mr Hyde had accepted that the law was on our side, more fool us. About four weeks later, I was in the kitchen early one evening when Cora called me from the sitting room. Cora and I know each other so well and I could tell she was terrified. I hurried through. She was standing by the window holding the corner of the curtains.

"'Someone is out there,' she said. 'Standing under the trees.'

"Our house is a large old Victorian building. In front is an unmade private road bordered on the other side by a high bushy hedge. Beyond this runs a row of large deciduous trees with low hanging branches. There is no street lighting. Together we peered out into the fading autumn evening. The leaves, though sere, were still mostly in place. At first I noticed nothing out of the ordinary, but as my eyes adjusted to the light I could pick out the unmistakable shape of a human head – large and shaggy – under the boughs. In the half-light the features were obscure, but we both knew who it was. He stood there motionless, staring at the house.

"Cora wanted to call the police, but what could we accuse him of – he was only standing there looking at his own house. There was no one whose help we could call on. Our few friends are old ladies like ourselves and we have no family living except a nephew in Scotland."

"We have each other, dear," said Cora reassuringly.

Letitia visibly brightened. "Yes, we have each other."

"We replaced the curtains and sat in silence in our sitting room for what seemed an age but was probably ten or fifteen minutes. The firm rap on the front door we both feared never came.

"'Is everything locked up at the back?' Cora had suddenly asked.

"'Surely he wouldn't come round there?' I'd said. He would have to climb the wall from the lane or come through the other gardens. I sounded more confident than I was and we both sprang up and hurried through to the kitchen.

"At the rear of the house is a large private garden bounded on two sides by the neighbouring gardens. The third boundary is a Victorian wall – eight feet or so high – bordering a narrow unmade lane wide enough for pedestrian access only, and used by the bin men and for garden access. We try to maintain it – we both love gardening."

"I won prizes in my youth when Reggie was alive," Cora interrupted.

"So you did, dear, but the garden is too large for us. We keep a flower bed near the house and a small lawn but the rest is substantially overgrown with large shrubs and trees. In the old days, Mr Rowe would come round and cut it back every few months, but Mr Hyde has done nothing. I suppose he would say it's our responsibility – which it probably is.

"Anyway there are two solid doors to the rear garden and both, to our immense relief, were firmly locked.

"So we returned to the sitting room and summoned up the courage to lift the curtain again. It was much darker now and the road, being private, is dimly lit, but we squinted into the light for several minutes before our initial sense that he was gone resolved itself into certainty."

"Perhaps he had merely been inspecting the condition of the house – it is his house after all. Perhaps we were foolish – foolish old women – to panic so. But panic we had and neither of us was relishing the long November night ahead.'

"But the night passed without incident and we awoke to a bright, crisp early winter day, and we both thought how stupid we had been and how sincerely relieved we were that we had not called the police."

"What do you think they would have said, Mr Gilbert? I'm sorry – Frank," asked Cora sheepishly.

"I think you were right to think they would have done nothing. They would have said he had committed no criminal offence and that it was a civil matter."

"Yes," said Cora. "That's exactly what they did say when we did eventually call them – after things had got much worse."

Letitia was now feeling that she ought to get to the crux of the matter.

"Nothing happened for a week or so. On the night of a spectacular full moon we went to bed in high spirits. We had enjoyed a wonderful production of *Turandot* on the radio."

"Do you know it, Mr – Frank?" interjected Cora. "It's by Puccini – it's our favourite."

"I certainly do, Cora – yes, it's terrific."

"Oh, I'm so pleased you're a Puccini fan. I am glad we chose you as our solicitor."

Realising that his irrelevant digression into Italian opera was down to her, Letitia pressed quickly on.

"Cora's bedroom on the first floor is at the back of the house and mine is next to it at the front. It seemed to me that my head had barely touched the pillow when I was roughly awoken by a series of prods to my shoulder and shaking of my arm. Cora was standing over me in her night dress – I have never seen her look more terrified.

"'What is it, dear? What's wrong?' I said to her.

"'Can't you hear it? It's horrible – listen, can't you hear it?'

"For a moment there was silence and then I heard it – the sound of a large dog howling, surprisingly close at hand.

"'It must be a neighbour's dog or some kids messing about.'

"'No, no,' hissed Cora. 'It's coming from our garden.'

"My spine tingled with that familiar feeling of icy water flowing down it – or blood freezing – I know it's a cliché but that's just what terror feels like.

"We knew we had to go into Cora's room and look out – perhaps it was a neighbour's dog, escaped into our garden. I looked at my clock – 2 am, the wee small hours, the witching hour. We knelt on the floor of Cora's room and we each lifted a corner of her heavy velvet curtains. The lawn looked bright in the full moon and for a moment there was silence. Then we saw the movement in the bushes at the bottom of the garden. How did the poet put it? 'What is that shape in the twisted trees?' – Auden, I think. We heard a low growl transform itself into the howl of a large dog. Had we not been in a back garden in the south Devon city of Plymouth we should have been in no doubt. It was the howl of a timber wolf – just as we had heard them on television wildlife programmes – calling to one another over vast expanses of Canadian snows. The howl died away, but in seconds it arose again. And as we stared transfixed and petrified towards the source, a large wolf's head emerged between the branches, raised its gaze heavenward and howled again at the full moon. Immediately lights came on in both the adjoining houses, a window opened, and the wolf's head withdrew back into the undergrowth and was silent."

Frank looked at Cora. She was in tears. Letitia too was visibly shaken. He wondered whether he should suspend the meeting and perhaps interview them again at the house in the new year to complete the statement. But no – that would only delay matters; they needed an early resolution and to achieve this, he needed to get an emergency legal aid certificate granted as soon as possible and the case into court before the Christmas break.

"Is there anything we can do about it? Will a court believe us?"

"I think you will be one of the most authentic and believable witnesses the court has seen, Letitia."

He had no doubt whatsoever that the local County Court judges would be immensely impressed with Letitia as a witness – her storyteller's skills, her mellifluous voice, and her patent honesty – but would also be moved by the evident vulnerability of herself and her sister.

If ever Frank had wanted to do his absolute best for his clients those clients were Cora and Letitia.

"But can you be certain it was Mr Hyde?"

"Yes we can, as it happened again the following night and this time we saw him quite clearly. The howling began at 2 am – we had not been able to sleep, we haven't really slept since. We peered around the curtains again, thinking he couldn't see us if our room was in darkness. But this time the wolf's head emerged from the undergrowth onto the lawn, followed on all fours by a large man's body. The body arched its back and howled again at the moon – half man half wolf, a horror from Germanic legend. And then the wolf's head tilted back – a very authentic mask – and looked straight at us. He could see us after all. His face distorted itself into a lupine snarl and then relaxed into a smug simian grin. Then he was gone, back into the undergrowth."

"And then this morning we received this in the post from a solicitor." Letitia produced a notice headed "Notice Seeking Possession of a Property Let on a Protected Shorthold Tenancy".

"And so we are here. If you can't help us, we will move out. But we love our home and we will be so upset if we have to leave. So, what rights do we have?"

Frank took a sip of his now-cold tea – mainly to gather his thoughts.

"Well, certainly you do have rights."

He glanced at the document Letitia had passed to him.

"And you needn't take any notice of this document either. Protected Shorthold Tenancies didn't come into existence until 1980. Your tenancy began before that and is a protected tenancy under the Rent Acts 1968 and 1977. To end it, your landlord needs to serve you with a valid Notice to Quit, which he hasn't done, and then apply to the county court for a possession order, which he won't get unless he can prove one of the grounds under the Rent Act. These mostly involve some fault by the tenant – such as not looking after the property or not paying the rent. Even if he could prove a Rent Act ground, which, as far as I am aware, he can't, the court would only grant him a possession order if he can convince the court that it's reasonable to do so. He would struggle with that given your age and how long you have lived there. If you are willing to stand up to him then I can't see any way he can lawfully evict you."

"But we can't afford to pay you," said Cora plaintively. "You have been ever so kind to see us today for free but…" She tailed off.

"It's called pro bono," said Letitia, trying not to look too pleased with herself. Frank nodded encouragingly.

"That won't matter," he said. "We will apply for legal aid to fund the defence of any possession claim and to apply for a court order to stop him harassing you – it's called an injunction."

"Will the court order him to stop howling like a wolf in the night?"

Frank smiled. "Under the Protection from Eviction Act, it is a criminal offence for a landlord to evict a residential tenant without a court order or to harass a tenant. I doubt the court will have come across a case where the harassment consists of pretending to be a werewolf. We may make a new legal precedent. You could be quoted in the law reports."

Cora looked delighted. Letitia didn't look so sure.

"So, what do we have to do next if we are going to stand up to him, as you put it?"

"Well, first I will prepare a statement for you to sign, Letitia." He had decided to avoid giving them the choice of whether Letitia or Cora would give evidence. "I will ring the Law Society to apply for an emergency legal aid certificate. The statement should be ready on Monday and, if it's convenient with you, I will pop round to see you at home to go through it and if you are happy you can sign it, Letitia. We might then be able to get into court next week."

"Gosh!" exclaimed Letitia and fell silent.

Frank was suddenly concerned that he might be allowing his own enthusiasm to run away with him.

"Or do you want the weekend to think things over? I could get a letter out to him today letting him know what he is doing is harassment and that he must stop immediately, failing which we will apply to the court for an injunction and an order that he pay the costs."

"I honestly don't think he would take any notice of a letter," said Cora. "And we would be afraid that he would be around to the house as soon as he received it. I think we are happy for you to go ahead with the court application."

She touched her sister's hand. "Aren't we, dear?"

"Yes, we are," Letitia replied confidently.

"Right then, is eleven on Monday morning convenient for you?"

They nodded.

"Good. I'll see you then and if he practises his wolf-man antics again over the weekend then by all means ring the police. I don't think they would be interested in a landlord standing looking at his house, but a werewolf in Mannamead? They might be. If he does, and you can get a photo, all the better. Merely pointing a camera at him might get rid of him." Frank could sense their concern that they would be on their own should Mr Hyde reappear at the weekend.

"But I am sure you will have no trouble this weekend – it's not a full moon." Did this sound flippant? He hoped not.

"Oh, and one last thing – I am not sure how friendly you are with your neighbours but it would help if you could speak with them to see what they heard or saw and whether they would be willing to give a statement. I could see them on Monday if they are. If you don't feel happy about that then I could write to them.

"Anyway, thank you for instructing me, try not to worry and I will see you on Monday."

Monday was a beautiful December day, cool, crisp and clear. Frank parked at the end of the private road. Frost sparkled on the hedgerow leaves as he strolled down to number four. It was an impressive house – one of a row of six in a Victorian terrace. Despite its exterior having that slightly down-at-heel look, typical of a rented property, he could immediately see why its landlord might want vacant possession. The area was in demand and most of the other houses in the row looked to have already undergone a process of re-gentrification, restoring them to their former glories as substantial professional family residences. He could see why Letitia and Cora loved living here. But Mr Hyde had bought subject to their protected tenancy and presumably had achieved a price reduction reflecting that. If he had not then more fool him. He would have to accept their right to live here for as long as they wished.

He rapped on the front door with the old brass knocker. The sitting room curtains twitched. The door quickly opened and both ladies stood in the porch, obviously delighted to see him.

They hurried him through to the sitting room and insisted he sat in their most comfortable chair. He noticed the threadbare nature of the carpets and much of the furniture. The pre-Raphaelite style fireplace, however, was spectacular, as was the high, ornately coved ceiling. Soon he was sipping Darjeeling from a bone china tea-cup, surrounded by a range of cakes.

"So, how was the weekend? Any problems?" he tentatively asked.

"No problems at all, Frank," replied Letitia. "A relaxing weekend. But, as you said, it wasn't a full moon. But we have been doing some research. We think Mr Hyde is a lycanthrope." She sat back looking pleased with herself.

"Right – I have a vague idea what that is but you'll need to expand."

"We have a friend – at our church – Edith. She is a retired psychologist. On Saturday we met her at the church coffee morning and told her all about Mr Hyde. We thought she wouldn't believe us but amazingly she said she had known a case like this before – a man who thought he was a wolf and behaved like one around the full moon. She told us there is a scientific word for it – lycanthropia, wolf madness, from the Greek *Lykos* for wolf and *Anthropos* for human being. It's an illness."

Alarm bells rang in Frank's mind.

"OK. I'm not sure if that helps us. We don't want the judge to think Mr Hyde is ill or suffering from a disability. We want the court to think he is bad – an unscrupulous landlord trying to terrify you into giving up your home of many years. We don't want to run any risk that the court might feel sorry for him – or order psychiatric reports."

Both women looked crestfallen.

"But don't worry – it's fascinating to know. We won't raise this ourselves but we'll know what Mr Hyde is talking about if he raises it as a defence.

"Anyway, let me tell you what I have been doing. We have legal aid to apply to the court for an injunction to stop him harassing you. This means you won't have to pay anything.

Also, here is the affidavit I have drawn up for you, Letitia. Please read it through carefully. Obviously, it needs to be true, and if there is anything you don't understand or want to change or add, let me know. If you're happy then I will arrange for you to visit a solicitor from a different firm to swear it – this just means that you sign it in their presence and swear that it's true – they will tell you what to say. Are you free to do that this afternoon?"

"Yes, that's fine, we don't have much to do except go to church! This will be a very busy week for us."

"I can then make the court application. The court is expecting it and can list it for hearing on Thursday morning at ten-thirty if you are happy for me to proceed?"

"I think we are, Letitia, aren't we, dear?"

"Yes, we are, but could we ask you a few questions?"

"Of course, Letitia, that's what I'm here for."

"First of all, will we need to say anything or will you do all the talking?"

"That depends on whether Mr Hyde wants to dispute any of your evidence. If he does, he or his advocate can ask you questions about it which you would have to answer on oath in the witness box. That might sound a bit scary, but it's nothing to worry about and it doesn't happen very often. Also, we might want to put him in the witness box for questioning."

"Thank you. Second question – do we have to tell Mr Hyde about the hearing? Does he have to be there?"

"He doesn't have to be there. It's up to him whether he turns up, but the court will expect us to give him notice of the hearing. I will ask a process server to personally serve him with the papers."

"We don't look forward to seeing him, but I suppose we have no choice. But what happens if the court makes the order we are asking for and he ignores it?"

"A good question – if he breaches the order he will be in contempt of court and can be sent to prison. The order will tell him that."

"He isn't going to like this, but what choice do we have? We can't spend our lives in mortal fear of our landlord," said Cora after a moment's hesitation.

Letitia took a moment to read through the affidavit and expressed herself happy. Frank was instructed to proceed, and, having made one last attempt to reassure them that nothing is ever as bad as you think it will be – not even court hearings – he arranged to meet them in the foyer at the County Court at 9.45 am on the coming Thursday.

The morning of the hearing came – dark and drizzly. As Cora and Letitia left for court by taxi, the sun seemed barely to have risen.

"A good day for wolves," remarked Letitia.

They were relieved to find Frank waiting for them at the court entrance, allaying their fear of an unsupported confrontation with Mr Hyde. Frank was struck by the old-fashioned elegance of their dress, two young society girls of the 1930s. His heart went out to them – this was a major event in their lives and he must not forget it. They had placed their total trust in his hands. Frank installed them in a comfortable interview room and went off to ask the usher to notify him if Mr Hyde or his representative turned up. The usher informed Frank that the court had received a letter from the defendant's solicitor and he disappeared to obtain a copy.

Frank reported back to his clients.

"The good news is that he isn't here and his solicitor has written to the court, so it may be that they won't be attending. Our process server personally served him with the papers – including a copy of your affidavit and notification of the hearing date – on Tuesday evening."

The usher appeared at the door with the solicitor's letter. Frank glanced through it as his clients looked on expectantly.

"Well, we are not the only ones who know about lycanthropia – let me read you this.

"My client suffers from a recognised mental disability known as lycanthropia, or wolf madness. The symptoms of this condition are an inclination, sometimes irresistible, to behave like a wolf at the time of the full moon. It is well documented through the centuries. My client admits the behaviour alleged, but denies that it was motivated by a desire to alarm or harass the Applicants. Rather, it is the manifestation of a mental illness, and as such the court should not subject him to an order which it may be medically impossible for him to comply with. I ask the court to excuse Mr Hyde's attendance at the hearing, which, given his psychological condition, might cause him profound emotional distress."

Momentarily both women were lost for words. Cora spoke first.

"His solicitor sounds just as clever as you, Frank. How could he concoct such nonsense and make it sound believable?"

"I wish the judge could have seen his face when he looked up at us from the bushes. Emotional distress – what drivel – he was enjoying every minute of it. He could terrify us into moving out and have a lot of sadistic fun at the same time. He would have made the perfect understudy for Oliver Reed in *The Curse of the Werewolf*. Will the judge believe any of this?" Cora continued.

"The judge is a retired circuit judge – Judge Peterson," Frank said. "He is a decent old chap and very experienced but it might be worth offering him some oral evidence from you, Letitia, confirming exactly what you just told me. Would you be happy with that?"

"Certainly," she replied. "If you think it will help." At that point, the usher appeared again at the door.

"You are first on. The court is ready."

"What do we call him, the judge?" said Letitia hurriedly.

"Your Honour. Stand up when he comes in, he and I will bow to each other but you don't need to. Sit down when he does and let me do the talking."

The women's nerves were partly relieved first by the modest, almost cosy, dimensions of the courtroom, and second by the fact that, as well as themselves, Frank and the judge, there was no one else in it but the usher and a smiling young woman sitting below the judge. They were also reassured by the kindly Pickwickian demeanour of the bewigged old gentleman who would decide their fate.

They sat down when he did. Frank remained standing and addressed the judge.

"Your Honour, I am Mr Gilbert and I appear for the Applicants."

The judge nodded in their direction.

"It may help Mr Gilbert if I confirm that I have read the papers fully, including the letter from the Defendant's solicitors. Have you seen that?"

"Yes, Your Honour."

"What do you say to it?"

"Firstly, Your Honour, it alleges a medical condition but there is no medical evidence in support. One would imagine that if Mr Hyde does genuinely suffer from such an unusual and debilitating condition, he would in the past have received treatment from a psychiatrist and would therefore be able to produce some supporting evidence."

"Perhaps there has been insufficient time?"

"Yes, perhaps, Your Honour, but they do not ask for time to seek such evidence or mention that treatment has been sought in the past. Secondly, Your Honour my clients are adamant that Mr Hyde's demeanour at the time suggested that he was quite enjoying the whole incident. This is referred to in paragraph three of the affidavit of Miss Clarke."

"Yes, I have seen that."

"Also, Your Honour, although I can't profess to having had any prior knowledge of this condition before this case, one would have thought that someone suddenly gripped by an irresistible impulse to howl at the full moon would do it in their own garden rather than jumping in the car and coming round to do it in the garden of their tenants."

From the flicker of a smile which passed across the judicial features at this point, Frank felt optimistic that the judge might be with him.

"Miss Clarke could give more detailed evidence regarding the Defendant's demeanour on the night in question, Your Honour, if that would assist?"

The judge reflected briefly.

"No, I don't think that will be necessary, Mr Gilbert. I am minded to grant your application, but to grant the

Defendant liberty to apply to discharge it if medical evidence is available."

"I am obliged, Your Honour. With a penal notice?"

"Yes, with a penal notice, but if this case does come back before the court for enforcement, I intend to leave a note on the file for my colleague hearing the case, that, in my view, should an application for committal be brought, the Defendant should be treated leniently if there is medical evidence before the court that the Defendant's impulsive behaviour was indeed irresistible.

"I therefore grant the injunction. I see your clients have a legal aid certificate and I don't propose to make any order for costs."

"I am obliged, Your Honour."

"Before I retire," said the judge, addressing Cora and Letitia directly, "may I say that I qualified as a barrister forty-four years ago and have been sitting as a judge for over twenty years and I have never before come across a case of lycanthropia. If I ever write my memoirs, this case will be in it. I am sorry that you had to be victims of it."

"Oh, good idea, Your Honour," said Cora coyly. "We will look forward to reading them."

Is she flirting with him? wondered Frank

The judge retired and Frank ushered his clients out of the courtroom and off to the canteen for a coffee.

"That wasn't too painful, was it?" he asked them.

"It wasn't painful at all – I almost enjoyed it," replied Cora. "And what a lovely judge."

"We now get the order drawn up and our process server will serve it, hopefully later today."

They embraced and parted at the door of the court after

Cora and Letitia had thanked him profusely. Frank promised to write to them to explain fully the events of the day and what they should do in the hopefully unlikely event of a breach of the order.

"Come back to me straight away if you have any problems, but most rational people comply with injunctions once it has been explained to them that they can be committed to prison for breach."

"Unless, of course, he really is a lycanthrope," said Letitia.

Frank heard nothing further regarding this case for several weeks. However, exactly four weeks after the hearing, he received a call from a Mrs Wilberforce, Mr Hyde's solicitor and the author of the letter produced at the hearing.

"Mr Gilbert? I represent Mr Hyde. Can we have an off-the-record chat?"

"Of course."

"I have instructions from Mr Hyde to serve notice to quit on your clients. We do of course acknowledge that the previous notice served by my client was invalid – those solicitors were not specialists in this field. The notice I serve will be valid and I then have instructions to issue possession proceedings."

This sounded like a negotiating tactic to Frank.

"You, no doubt, are a specialist in this field, Mrs Wilberforce. So you will be aware that my clients have a protected tenancy under the Rent Act. What possible grounds can your client have for possession?"

"We will seek possession under Cases 3 and 4 of Schedule 15 of the Rent Act 1977. Your clients have allowed the interior of the premises and the furniture to deteriorate over many years."

"That is nonsense, Mrs Wilberforce. I have been to the property. The condition is not bad and any disrepair would fall within your client's repairing obligations."

"Well, that will be for the court to decide, but hear me out, Mr Gilbert. My client is a sensitive soul."

Frank resisted the urge to guffaw audibly.

"He does not want to cause unnecessary stress either to himself or your clients. He is willing to offer your clients a substantial sum to surrender their tenancy. He will offer them the sum of five thousand pounds – payable on the usual basis that is he will deposit it with me and I will undertake to pay it to you when they have vacated."

"I don't think for a moment they will be interested. They love their home – they have lived there for nearly twenty years. Even if they were minded to move, that sum isn't nearly enough to compensate them for the loss of the very valuable rights they have as protected tenants. Any new tenancy they take will of course be an assured tenancy – probably a shorthold."

"Yes, yes, I understand, but we think it's a reasonable offer – taking into account their age and the fact that they have no one to whom they can transmit the tenancy. So please take instructions."

Frank said he would do. He would advise them not to accept, that the threat of possession proceedings was bluff and that obtaining vacant possession of a house of this size in this location against a protected tenant would be worth far more than five thousand pounds to Mr Hyde.

Frank did not immediately put this proposal to his clients as he was due in court. However, on returning to the office later in the day, a message awaited him to ring Letitia. He wondered if she knew of the offer. She didn't, however, and the news she gave him came as quite a surprise.

"We are terribly sorry, Frank, and we feel guilty that we are wasting all the wonderful work you did for us, but Cora and I have decided to move out. We have not felt comfortable here since the hearing and it doesn't feel like home anymore with Mr Hyde as our landlord. I realised I felt like this after only a few days, but didn't want to raise it with Cora. When I did so, I was relieved to find that she felt exactly the same. A friend at our church owns a nice little terraced house which has just become available to rent, much smaller and easier to look after. We have looked at it and agreed to take it. You aren't too annoyed with us, are you?"

"No, no, of course not," Frank laughed. "It's obviously your decision. If you will feel safer and happier there then I completely understand and my work may not have been wasted. Have you told Mr Hyde yet?"

"No, we don't want anything to do with him. We were hoping you would."

"That's good. By coincidence I received a call from Mr Hyde's solicitor this morning. She offered five thousand pounds if you would give up your tenancy. I was going to advise you to refuse, but obviously this changes things completely. What I advise now is that you instruct me to go back to him and say you would accept seven thousand five hundred pounds, plus your legal fees, otherwise the Legal Aid Authority may take a chunk of your money to recoup their outlay."

"No, Frank, we don't want anything from him. We just want to be rid of him and we will pay your fees."

"I am not annoyed with you for 'wasting all my wonderful

work', as you put it, but I hope you won't mind if I reserve the right to be annoyed with you if you look a gift horse in the mouth and walk away with nothing. At least let me go back to them and accept the five thousand pounds."

Letitia chuckled like a naughty girl. "All right, we wouldn't want you to be annoyed with us. Let me just discuss it with Cora."

Letitia and Cora accepted the offer and six weeks later moved into their new accommodation with money in their pockets and a landlord who didn't think he was a werewolf. With appropriate alterations of names and addresses, Frank dined out on the werewolf story for many years, and considered himself the premier authority on lycanthropy in the local legal profession.

Part Two

The Piglet Rustler of Penwith

Some weeks after the resolution of the werewolf case, Frank was sitting in his office late one afternoon when a welcome face appeared around the door.

"Pub, Sir Humphrey?"

"Be there in ten minutes. Just one pint though. I'm in the Penwith magistrates' court at 10 am tomorrow."

The welcome face belonged to Frank's boss, the partner in charge of the firm's Plymouth office, Dick Guildford-Brown. A former Army captain, accomplished raconteur and committed party animal, Dick was a bit of a celebrity among the local estate agents and financial advisers. Some of the more formal members of the local legal profession muttered darkly that he did not always take his role as legal professional and officer of the Supreme Court as seriously as it deserved. But if you were an introducer of business to local solicitors' firms, touting for an invitation to a business lunch, his was the invitation you wanted.

Thirty minutes later, Frank threw the last of the faxed

statements for tomorrow's hearing into his briefcase, locked the office and skipped the few steps down the road to the Minster. Dick sat alone at the bar, already on his second beer.

"Monday evening, always dead in here on a Monday evening."

He sounded crestfallen. He functioned better with an audience.

"Here, drink this, Sir Humphrey." Dick lovingly caressed a pint of golden IPA along the bar in Frank's direction.

"Why do you call him Sir Humphrey?" a voice enquired from below the bar. Dick was a keen student of maritime history and, like many ex-servicemen, had a passion for nicknames.

"Sir Humphrey Gilbert – redoubtable Elizabethan sea-faring chap of these parts and, for all we know, a frequenter of the Barbican pubs and an ancestor of Frank's."

"That explains it then." The voice now appearing above the bar belonged to Bernard the landlord, an ex-naval man and a sympathetic confidante to the solitary drinker.

"What are you doing in darkest Penwith?" asked Dick.

"I seem to be defending a man charged with the theft of a piglet."

Dick beamed pleasantly. "Piglet rustling – a classic west Cornish crime. Where did that one come from?"

"Alan Bradshaw rang me this afternoon. Until lunchtime he was doing it himself, but he's double booked. So I get two working hours' notice. And why has he chosen the least experienced lawyer in the firm?"

Alan Bradshaw was a partner in one of the firm's Cornish offices, a bluff, fifty-something Yorkshireman and one of

Cornwall's premier criminal advocates. Unlike most of the other lawyers in the firm, he was a specialist, undertaking nothing but criminal work throughout the far-flung magistrates' courts of the county and much sought after by the Cornish criminal community. Frank dreaded to think how disappointed his client was going to be when he realised that he had turned up and not Alan.

"He chose you because the rest of us are all conveyancers – you remember criminal law from law school – and anyway, didn't you do it in your articles at Chamberlains?"

"Yes some, not much – about three months."

"You'll be terrific, you'll knock 'em dead, old chum."

Frank was still rereading the statements spread out on the passenger seat and occasionally balanced on his steering wheel as he drove across the Goss Moor through sheets of Celtic drizzle the following morning.

It seemed that local farmers had been the victim of a series of piglet thefts. Frank was unsure if there was any technical difference between a pig or piglet other than age and size. The essential element seemed to be that all the animals stolen were small enough for an adult to stash away under the arm and run off with. Some of the stolen piglets had been recovered – wandering aimlessly in the local village – but others had disappeared without trace.

Alan Bradshaw had warned Frank that the defendant, Caleb Carter, appeared at first instance to be "not very bright". But Alan suspected that he was much cleverer than he let on. He seemed to be highly amused by the court process. Frank felt slightly unsettled at how well Alan, a prolific criminal lawyer, seemed to know the defendant.

The evidence against Carter essentially consisted of a single eye-witness statement from a respected local shopkeeper who claimed to have clearly seen the defendant running down the deserted village fore street late one evening with a piglet under his arm (Tom, Tom, the piper's son references seemed inevitable). There was further evidence of a highly suspect police interview in which the defendant claimed that at the time of the alleged offence he was on his way back from his book club. Frank could see why Alan believed that Carter was brighter than he seemed. Could he have been having a bit of fun at the expense of the investigating officer?

Frank arrived at the old court house in good time. The Gothic-looking town hall built of characteristic Cornish granite in the early Victorian era doubled up as the local magistrates' court. The day was, if anything, even gloomier in this west Cornish seaside town than in the central Cornish moorland through which he had driven. Nothing boded well.

He entered the foyer and asked the usher if the defendant had arrived.

"You mean old Caleb? No, he's not here yet. He'll be on time though – never keeps the court waiting."

This was not going well. Alan Bradshaw had assured Frank that his client would meet him at least forty-five minutes beforehand. This would only be Frank's second attempt at conducting a summary criminal trial on his own. Alan had done hundreds and the prospect of extemporising on the hoof might not intimidate him.

Frank, on the other hand, was fully aware that the only substitute for vast experience or innately brilliant advocacy, neither of which he possessed, was in-depth preparation, the opportunity for which he had now been deprived of. He contemplated impending disaster – his reputation destroyed before he had one. And, it was in open court – other advocates might sit in the back of the court and snigger at his naive unpreparedness. The local press might report his ineptitude.

What was more, his client was plainly on first-name terms with the usher and a regular at the Penwith magistrates' court. It was inadmissible for the prosecution to influence the court with evidence of previous criminal behaviour, but if his client was already well known to the Justices then what hope did he have?

He looked at his watch – ten to ten. His musings were interrupted by a sharp knock on the door of the interview room in which he had hoped to spend time with his client forensically picking apart the witness statements.

It was opened by the usher.

"Here's your brief, Caleb – Mr…?"

"Mr Gilbert," said Frank.

"Thank'ee kindly, Bob," came the reply from around the door and a short stocky figure, entirely engulfed in a green gabardine raincoat of tent-like proportions, topped by a large pointed sou'wester dripping with rain, loomed into view.

"Very pleased to meet you, Mr Carter. I am afraid Mr Bradshaw can't represent you today. He is busy in the Crown Court."

Frank braced himself for the storm.

"Don't 'ee worry 'bout that, Mr Gilbert. Mr Bradshaw says you be much cleverer than 'e is."

As he said this, Caleb swept off his sou'wester and Frank was confronted by the round, ruddy, beaming face of a man in his fifties, balding at the front but with long, straggly, slightly hippy-ish locks at the back and sides.

His eyes twinkled with mischief and such a look of unrestrained glee that Frank wondered whether he detected irony. But at least Caleb was not appalled by the absence of Cornwall's finest, and his replacement by Cornwall's greenest.

Anyway, time was running out. They could be on in five minutes.

"So, Mr Carter, your defence is, it was not you – a case of mistaken identity – you were somewhere else – at your book club?"

"I could tell you were clever. You know the case inside out already, you got it exactly."

"Well, they are going to ask you questions about that – or perhaps the police already have?" Frank realised he should know this. "Have you been to the book club before?"

"No, this was the first time."

"Where is it?"

"Mouzzole. It's the Mouzzole book club for farmers and fishermen – no toffs allowed – no in'ellectles."

"No what?"

"In'ellectles – you know – blokes like you."

Frank now reached the question which he had no doubt would blow Caleb's alibi out of the water when the prosecution asked it.

"And what were you reading?"

"*Lady Chatlee's Lover*."

With that, Bob the usher peered around the door.

"You're on."

Frank's heart sank.

"I think we should ask the clerk for a short delay – twenty minutes should do."

He at least needed to finish reading the papers and explain to his client how ridiculous his alibi would sound. As if reading his mind, Caleb interrupted.

"Don't worry. I ain't relying on that alibi no more, so we don't need no delay – let's get on with it. I got darts in The Pilchard at lunchtime."

And before Frank could remonstrate, his client was gone out of the door, across the foyer and through the imposing double doors into what he assumed was the courtroom. Frank had no choice but to follow, and, as he frantically reassembled the case papers, he could only hope that the substantial portion that he had not yet read contained nothing vital to the case.

The courtroom was empty but for a woman in her early thirties sitting below the bench – the court clerk. It was her job to advise the magistrates on the law and ensure the conduct of the trial was procedurally correct.

Frank nodded in her direction.

"Mr Gilbert?"

"Yes, that's me."

"Is this still a not-guilty plea?"

The Crown prosecutor now appeared and took up her place beside Frank.

"Jane Williams," she said to Frank and they shook hands.

"It is," said Frank, addressing both the clerk and the prosecutor. "My client says he was elsewhere – it was not him."

"OK, I will call Their Worships."

Frank glanced around at Caleb. The laughter in his eyes

was alarming – how could he be enjoying this? He was being tried for a criminal offence.

The door opened at the back of the court.

"The court will rise," boomed Bob the usher.

Caleb was already on his feet – he knew the ropes.

Three people entered the court after the clerk and took up their positions along the bench. They bowed in the direction of the advocates, who bowed back. They all sat except Caleb. He did not need to be told to remain standing while the clerk read the charge.

"Do you plead guilty or not guilty?"

"Not guilty," said Caleb with gusto and then followed this up with a cheery smile. "Good morning, Major Andrew, sir, bleak weather we're 'aving," he said before sitting down.

Frank looked round in surprise. Caleb was beaming in the direction of the Chairman of the Bench.

The clerk immediately intervened.

"Mr Carter, if you want to address the Chairman of the Bench, please do it through your solicitor, unless you are invited to address him direct, in which case please refer to him as 'Your Worship' or 'Sir' – not Major Andrew."

"Sorry, Ma'am," beamed Caleb, not in the least taken aback.

The prosecutor then rose and made the opening address. She explained that on the evening in question at about 11.30 pm, a local farmer, a Mr Dawe, had been awoken by a disturbance in the piggery. The occupants were obviously unsettled. He had peered out into the stormy November night, and through the heavy rain he thought he could just discern a shadow disappearing through the gate from the piggery yard. Mr Dawe was in his seventies and did not fancy giving chase or even getting drenched by going to investigate at that unearthly hour.

When he did investigate the next morning, a three-month-old piglet was missing, the fourth he had lost over the last few years. He had reported the matter to the police, expecting very little. He was pleasantly surprised, therefore, to hear that the police had a suspect.

The second prosecution witness would be a Mr William Trout, a fifty-something shopkeeper. He had been walking home from his local pub in the nearby village of Penworzel, a mile and a half or so from the scene of the crime. He had turned a corner and was astounded to be confronted by the figure of a man wearing a sou'wester careering down the street carrying a piglet under his arm. The figure had looked straight at him and, appearing to recognise him, had swerved off into a side street and disappeared from view. Despite the darkness and pouring rain, Mr Trout was clear as to the identity of the running figure. It was the defendant, who Mr Trout knew well as a bit of a local character. He immediately rang the police and reported the incident.

At 10 am the following morning, the police had attended at the defendant's cottage and asked the defendant where he had been the previous evening. The defendant had said he was at his book club. He had immediately been arrested on suspicion of the theft of a piglet.

The defendant had subsequently admitted that the book club claim was, as he put it, "a bit of drollery", relieving the police of the need to identify and interview other members of the book club (this was news to Frank, but at least he would not now need to put this preposterous alibi before the court). He still firmly denied the offence, however.

It was now for the prosecution to call its evidence. After a brief consultation with his client, Frank informed the court that he was happy for the evidence of Mr Dawe and the investigating police officers to be read to the court without cross examination. All it proved was that a piglet had been stolen and that Caleb denied having done it. True, it might also suggest that Caleb was not averse to a bit of tomfoolery at the expense of the police, but this was not what he was charged with. It might also undermine his credibility as a reliable witness in the eyes of the magistrates if and when he came to give evidence. But first the prosecution had to prove its case.

So, only the shopkeeper, William Trout, was to give evidence. He entered the witness box, a stout, ruddy-faced gentleman who, Frank suspected, could be found staggering home from his local on many evenings similar to the night in question. There was a word to describe his appearance – what was it? "Rhino-haemorrhagic", that was it, but he would keep quiet about that. Nothing was to be gained by insulting the witness.

Mr Trout took his oath with an air of pomposity, and the prosecutor then took him quickly through his evidence. He confirmed his certainty that the figure he had witnessed carrying the piglet was the defendant. No doubt the prosecutor, despite her youthful appearance, had handled many more such trials than he had, but Frank felt she had placed insufficient emphasis on the proximity of the witness to the defendant – seventy-five feet, according to his statement – and the witness claimed to be a close acquaintance. Perhaps there was some slim hope to be found here.

He scribbled some quick notes and then stood up to

begin his cross examination – for the second time ever in a criminal court.

"Mr Trout, can you tell the court, with as much accuracy as possible, what time you saw the figure carrying the piglet?"

"Oh, about ten-thirty, I should say."

"And you had just left The Moon and Hedgehog?"

"That's right."

"At what time had you arrived at The Moon and Hedgehog?"

"About eight."

"Can I suggest that it might have been rather later that you saw the running figure?"

"No, it was ten-thirty."

Somewhere, in his occasional reading about the techniques of good advocacy, he recalled that the job of a cross-examiner could be facilitated by those witnesses prone to adopting dogmatic certainty at the merest hint of contradiction. It seemed that Mr Trout was such a witness.

"But, Mr Trout, we have already heard the prosecution state that the theft took place an hour later, at around eleven-thirty. If the person you say you witnessed was the perpetrator, then, as he was carrying a piglet, he couldn't have crossed your path until closer to midnight. Unless you witnessed the perpetrator of some other earlier piglet theft?"

Frank was pleased with this line but tried not to show it. He heard an audible chuckle behind him.

"Of course not – that's stupid. There was only one theft. It must have been a bit later," Mr Trout conceded. "Anyway, what difference does it make?"

"The difference, Mr Trout, is that at ten-thirty the pub lights were on and lights would have been on in most of the cottages. At midnight there would be none.

"So, you were in the pub for nearly four hours. You stayed until closing time and for a very generous drinking up time thereafter. How much did you drink?"

"I dunno – three pints, four?"

"Any shorts?"

"One whiskey."

"OK, a fair bit then. It was very dark, wasn't it?"

"Pretty dark."

"All the lights were out?"

"Yes, except the street light."

"It was raining heavily?"

"Yes."

"So, there would have been no starlight or moonlight?"

"No, but there was still the street light."

"How far were you from the running figure?"

Mr Trout replied quickly and confidently.

"About seventy-five yards."

Frank hesitated momentarily. He glanced at Mr Trout's statement, as he thought it stated that the distance was seventy-five feet. He looked across at the prosecutor who was writing furiously. Had she noticed? Surely she would correct this in a re-examination of her witness.

Frank decided to emphasise the point.

"Seventy-five yards, you say?"

No sooner had the words left his lips, he realised he had committed a "rookie error". Was it Sir David Napley's instruction manual on advocacy skills, *The Technique of Persuasion*, which advised the inexperienced advocate never to allow an opposing witness the opportunity to correct a material error?

But once again, fortune was with him.

"Yes, seventy-five yards, I said."

Frank swiftly ended his examination. "No further questions," and sat down.

He waited with bated breath to see if the prosecutor would take the opportunity to re-examine the witness on the question of proximity to the suspect. She did not.

"That completes the case for the prosecution," she said.

It was now for Frank to present the defendant's case.

From their first encounter, Frank had not been relishing Caleb's appearance in the witness box. He would be asked about his ridiculous alibi, why he had given it, why he had withdrawn it and what he had in fact been doing on the night in question. His obvious amusement at the whole procedure and his casual carefree demeanour would not endear him to the court.

"Can I have a quick word with my client?" Frank asked the court.

They conferred briefly. "Yes, of course, Mr Gilbert."

"We're doing pretty good, ain't we?" said Caleb, as the court doors swung to behind them as they left the court.

"Well, possibly, and I don't want to undo our good work, so I suggest you don't give evidence."

"What, not go into the box?" Caleb looked profoundly disappointed. "I have to tell 'em I never done it and what I was doing."

What that might have been, he didn't expand on.

"It's not for us to prove you didn't do it, Mr Carter. It's for the prosecution to prove you did – and arguably they haven't done that. If you don't go into the box, then apart from my closing speech, the case is over.

"If you do give evidence, the prosecution can cross-examine you, and who knows where that may lead."

Caleb thought for a moment.

"OK, if that's what you advise. Though I would 'ave made an excellent witness, I always do."

The court and prosecutor seemed surprised when Frank announced that the defence would produce no evidence. He had no idea how often this happened in the magistrates' – he hoped he had not committed a major error.

Frank stood to deliver his closing speech. He began at last to feel more relaxed. He knew he was no great shakes at cross-examination – he suspected he never would be. But he thought he could make a passable attempt at a closing speech especially where, as here, he had something worthwhile to say.

"Your Worships. There is no dispute that on the night in question, a piglet was stolen from Mr Dawe's farm. The only evidence produced by the prosecution that the defendant was responsible is the identification evidence of one witness alone – Mr Trout."

He paused briefly to finger open the large legal tome he had brought with him – *Archbold: Criminal Pleading Evidence and Practice* – the bible of criminal lawyers. Finding things in such magisterial legal works was notoriously difficult, but to his relief the book virtually fell open at the page he wanted.

"Your Worships will no doubt be familiar with the Court of Appeal decision in 'R v. Turnbull'?" He doubted they were, but a little flattery couldn't hurt.

The clerk now found the relevant page in her edition of *Archbold* – just in case the devious advocate had it in mind to lead Their Worships up the garden path.

"In that case, the court laid down that where the prosecution was seeking to achieve a conviction based on the evidence of a single eye-witness alone, the judge should direct the jury – or in a magistrates' court trial, the magistrates should direct themselves – of the need to take particular care before convicting. In doing so, the court should carefully consider the circumstances of the identification, such as, how long did the observation last, at what distance, in what light and" – Frank would have liked to have been able to omit this latter point – "whether or not the witness knew the defendant.

"In the Turnbull case, the defendant was actually convicted, but the witness, a police officer who knew the defendant, was only ten yards away. In this case, as you have heard, the witness says he was seventy-five yards away." He moved on quickly.

"It was late November, the darkest day of the year." He thought this was a line from a poem but couldn't remember which. "It was midnight. The village lights would be out, except, as you have heard, for one street light. It was raining heavily with no moonlight or starlight. The perpetrator was running and wearing a sou'wester." He immediately wished he hadn't said this, in case any of the magistrates had seen the defendant arriving at the court in his sou'wester.

"A day, very much like today, in fact," he continued. "It would be very hard to identify anyone at seventy-five yards in the light we have in the street now – and it is eleven o'clock in the morning, not midnight.

"In my submission, Your Worships, you cannot be sure, given the guidelines in the Turnbull case, that it was the defendant who the witness saw that evening. And if you are not sure then, as that is the only evidence against the defendant, he is entitled to be acquitted."

Frank thanked the magistrates for listening to him and they then retired to consider their verdict. He was fairly sure they would convict. If they looked again at Mr Trout's witness statement, they would see the original distance of seventy-five feet. He had been sure of the defendant's identity and claimed to know him well and, even though the defendant was perfectly entitled to decline to give evidence and leave it to the prosecution to prove its case, Frank expected the magistrates to take a dim view of his unwillingness to enter the witness box and to draw adverse conclusions.

It was then that he realised that amongst the papers he had not had time to read was a document headed "R v. Carter – Antecedents" – a list of the defendant's previous convictions. Frank had no doubt that he had some and, if Caleb was convicted, Frank would need to try to explain these away, if that was possible.

But he had no time. The magistrates were back – was this good or bad?

The magistrates resumed their seats on the bench. The clerk re-announced the case and Caleb stood up.

"Your Worships, do you find the defendant guilty or not guilty of the charge of theft of a piglet?"

The Chairman looked balefully, it seemed to Frank, in Caleb's direction.

"Mr Carter, the court finds you not guilty of the charge. You are free to go."

"Thankee very much, Major Andrew, sir, and to your colleagues – a just decision, sir," said Caleb and looked as if he were about to advance in their direction and shake hands.

The clerk was again about to intervene, but Frank decided this was probably his role and placed a gentle restraining hand on his client's shoulder and ushered him out of the court.

"Thank 'ee kindly, Mr Gilbert. You'm just as clever as Mr Bradshaw said you were. I shall tell 'm 'ow clever you are and ask 'im to make sure I gets you next time."

Frank began to think he was exaggerating the Cornish brogue.

"Is it too much to hope that there won't be a next time?"

Caleb was delighted by this comment and responded with a wholehearted belly laugh. It was obviously much too stupid a suggestion to deserve a reply.

They shook hands and parted – Frank to his car for his long journey across the rain-soaked Cornish moors and Caleb to the cosy tavern just around the corner for an afternoon of beer and darts.

Frank arrived back in the office in the early afternoon. Just before close of business, he received a call from Alan Bradshaw.

"So, what did he get, community service, probation? Or perhaps he was already on a suspended?"

"He was acquitted," replied Frank, with more than a touch of pride.

"What, seriously? Far be it from me to doubt your forensic skills, but how did that happen? They would have known he had done it."

"Well, they obviously didn't know that, and he told me he hadn't and you told me it was a not guilty."

Frank related the morning's events, making efforts to downplay the howler dropped by the prosecution star witness and give the impression that skill and not luck had carried the day.

"Well, keeping him out of the box was a good call, but they still knew he'd done it."

"How?"

"He's a bit of a folk hero in the area – a notorious piglet rustler. He has several convictions for it. He steals from the richer gentleman farmers and offers them to the poorer ones. If, as usually happens, they won't take them, he releases them back near the farms they came from. The Piglet Rustler of Penwith, they call him."

Frank was speechless.

"Why didn't you tell me?" he eventually spluttered.

"You had his antecedents."

"I never had the time to read them."

"How would it have helped? If, as he usually does, he wanted to plead not guilty – which he did – it wouldn't have helped. But good result anyway," he said, moving quickly on. "I know I can trust you with these short-notice ones in future."

Great, thought Frank, dejectedly, but said nothing.

"Incidentally, who was the Chairman of the Bench?"

"A Major Andrew. Caleb seemed to know him well."

"Ah, George Andrew – a gentleman farmer of the area. Yes, Caleb does know him. He stole a piglet from him last year."

Part Three

The Case of the Stolen Charity Box

As most experienced police officers will know, a significant percentage of minor crimes in any particular locality are committed by a small number of persistent offenders. Certain individuals – the kleptomaniac Artful Dodgers of the modern world – are responsible for hundreds of minor thefts; opportunistically preying on the careless, the inattentive and the trusting in the apparent belief that this constitutes a worthy and respectable occupation much like any other.

Frank had one such client. Still in his late teens, Lee Facey, afterthought of the redoubtable Mrs Molly Facey, matriarch of a long line of petty and not so petty criminals, had already, by his nineteenth birthday, accumulated a string of convictions for theft running to several sheets of a police antecedents list.

Frank did not really relish the prospect of defending major career criminals, which some of Lee's older brothers undoubtedly were. Lee, on the other hand, you couldn't help liking. Genial, good-humoured and seemingly always immensely grateful for your efforts on his behalf, Frank often thought what a good salesman he could have been with a little education, a little smartening up and different parents.

Invariably when he visited the office, skinny, scruffy, spiky-haired and beaming, he came bearing gifts. Wines, spirits, perfume, even watches – which to Frank's untutored eye looked way beyond Lee's legitimate price range – were showered on the staff who anticipated his appointments with mounting excitement. The office's three secretaries would desert their typing stations in the back office to compete with the two reception staff for their share of the spoils. No-one was left disappointed.

Frank and his boss Dick agonised over whether to allow the staff to accept these gifts. Could they be accepting stolen property? Lee was in receipt of income support and had no discernible means of lawfully dispensing such largesse. And Frank had defended him on charges of theft of items very similar to those he was giving away. But the staff were delighted, had no other perks of the job and the decision was delayed; so the gifts continued.

No-one denied that he was possessed of a warm and generous nature. He did not use his ill-gotten gains to acquire the trademark large black BMW so beloved of petty criminals. Instead, part Robin Hood, part Artful Dodger, he disbursed largesse to those he felt best deserved it.

But bizarrely this did not prevent him from stealing from the very same people. Theft was a way of life. Anything in the office, portable and capable of concealment about the person was safely stashed away before his visits. Things had still gone missing at around the time of his appointments. The office receptionists hotly disputed that Lee was responsible, but nothing went missing at any other time. No one saw him do it, but then he was a professional.

On a sparkling late afternoon one Thursday in April, Frank and Dick were at their usual place at the Minster bar, contemplating their first pint of the evening. Both double doors were open and a gentle spring breeze wafted through the bar. With them were two other local businessmen, Vic Gibbs, a radiantly bald cockney financial adviser in his late thirties, and George Barker, a laconic pipe-smoking chartered surveyor a few years his senior.

Spirits were running high, as although all four were regulars at the Minster, this evening's meeting had a specific purpose. Tomorrow they were taking the overnight ferry crossing to Roscoff. Dick, a staunch Francophile and regular user of Brittany Ferries cross-channel services, had already arranged the whole thing and no further discussion was strictly necessary. Anticipation of the trip was as pleasurable as the trip itself and they sank a couple of pints each before they could agree what they all knew anyway, namely, that they would reconvene at the Quiberon bar at midnight the next day.

"What a Shakespearean treat I've got in store for you all tomorrow," Vic exclaimed, grinning smugly. "You're going to hear Shakespearean English as she was meant to be spoke; not your John Gielgud public-school version." He waved dismissively in Dick's direction.

Dick was a popular public-house thespian, an accomplished mimic and master of accents with a repertoire renowned amongst local boozers – *Henry V*'s Agincourt scene, *Richard II*'s "This England" speech, "The Owl and the Pussy-Cat", "Albert and the Lion" – a vast and varied range.

And Vic could not resist joining in, contrasting Dick's classic diction with his broad cockney.

"But will you get the words right?" asked George. "It's no good making it up as you go along."

Vic cleared his throat and adopted the pose of an accomplished tragedian.

"We few, we 'appy few, we band of bruvvers.

For he today that sheds his blood with me

Shall be my bruvver be he ne'er so vile."

In ending he attempted rather clumsily the theatrical genuflection of an Elizabethan courtier.

"What do you think of that then, oh ye of little faith?" he called over his shoulder as he and George drifted off to join a rowdy group of drunken estate agents.

"I see you had our young friend Lee in earlier," said Dick. "What's he been up to now?"

"I'm in court with him tomorrow – Dartbridge magistrates'. He is charged with stealing the charity collection box from the Dartbridge Hotel."

"What, that lovely old coaching inn? Does an excellent pint of draft bass?"

"That's the one."

"I should have thought he would have stood out like a sore thumb in that place – wouldn't fit in with the county set."

"I agree, but he never seems to take into account the chances of being caught."

"Is he owning up?"

"Well, he admits he took it. But he seems to have picked up some smatterings of criminal law in his numerous court appearances. He claims he always intended to give it back and so there was no intention to permanently deprive."

"Did he bring it back?"

"No. The police picked him up in his old Wartburg as he was driving back to Plymouth. They were tipped off by a regular, some retired colonel, who saw him take it and followed him outside. No car that decrepit has ever been seen in Dartbridge so the good colonel had no problem in describing it."

"So what is he pleading?"

"Not guilty he says at the moment, though I need a longer chat with him about that."

"OK. Well, good luck with that one."

"I'll go straight to court in the morning, so see you about lunch time when, incidentally, I won't be drinking even though it's Friday. My next drink will be on the ferry. I want to look forward to it."

Friday morning, blue-skied and radiant, found Frank driving contentedly through the rolling green hills of the South Hams countryside. The roads snaked circuitously through the little South Devon villages between Plymouth and Dartbridge. The rolling English drunkard who built the rolling English road would have been proud of these.

He arrived in the ancient river valley market town in good time for his nine-thirty meeting. The river Dart, one of Devon's major rivers, tumbled down from the foothills of Dartmoor a few miles to the north, and could become a roaring torrent after heavy rain on the moors. Today, however, it meandered, a glistening ribbon, through the water meadows below the ruins of Dartbridge's Norman motte-and-bailey castle and into the old town.

To his relief he quickly found a space in the court car park. He noticed his client's ancient and, he was sure,

49

unroadworthy vehicle standing unashamedly right outside the court entrance in the space reserved for magistrates.

He was now getting to know the ushers in the local courts and exchanged a pleasant greeting with Ioain, a genial Welsh rugby fanatic who had apparently played the game to a decent level in his youth.

"Fine morning, Mr Gilbert, are you representing Mr Facey?"

"I have that pleasure."

"I have put him in Interview Room 2. He seems a jolly fellow."

"Thank you, Ioain – and please call me Frank. I'm afraid his jollity may not go down so well with the magistrates when they hear what he's charged with."

"OK, Lee," said Frank once he had emptied his briefcase over the table of Interview Room 2. He knew he must appear decisive.

"Are you still saying you want to plead not guilty?"

"Yep. I took it but I never meant to keep it. If the fuzz hadn't stopped me I'd have brung it back."

"So where do you say you were taking it?"

"To Plymouth."

"And in the wholly unlikely event that they ask you why you were doing that, what will you say?"

"I was goin' to make a big donation from money I got at home."

This begged a number of questions.

"So then they might ask you why you needed to take the box to Plymouth. Wouldn't it have been easier to bring the money to the box?"

Lee pondered for a moment.

"Well first, I never thought of that, and second, I was collectin' some more donations. I know some very gen'rous people in Plymouth who don't often come up round these parts."

Frank had a pretty good idea of the sort of people Lee knew in Plymouth and he suspected the investigating police officer might know them too.

"You see, Lee, the court might think that most people considering removing the charity box from the hotel to collect more funds would have asked for permission."

"I did think of that, but the barman was a posh git and I thought he wouldn't believe I would bring it back."

Frank thought that the court wouldn't believe this either, but said nothing. He decided to adopt a different approach.

"The statement of Sergeant Crooke says that when they recovered the box it had only seven pounds in it and all in coins."

"Ha ha, Sergeant Crooke – can't you change his name for him by one of those deeds? It's me who should be called that!"

Frank suppressed a chuckle. The last thing he wanted to do was encourage the comedian in his client.

"Come on, be serious." He smiled.

"So what are you saying? That's how much was in it?"

"But the statement from the hotel manager says that the box had been there over three weeks and when it is emptied at the end of each month it usually holds a few hundred pounds and mostly in notes."

"Well, I didn't take it. The barman must 'ave. Anyway, they searched me and the car. They didn't find nothin'."

"So, if they ask you if you came up with any friends who went back separately with the dosh?"

"I'll say no – 'cos I didn't. They ain't got no evidence of that, have they?"

"Colonel Hall's statement said that he thought he had seen the perpetrator walk away up Fore Street with two other young men, but could not be certain that they were together."

"But they won't ask me any of this today, will they, if I pleads not guilty? They'll just put it off to another day because their witnesses won't be here and we can all go home."

"Well, that's true, but if we all come back again in four weeks' time and you use up half a day of court time telling them what you've just told me and they don't believe you, then with your previous convictions you run the risk of a prison sentence even if you did only steal seven pounds. They don't like thefts from charities."

"You think they won't believe me?"

"I'm afraid to say I do. On the other hand, if you plead guilty today, it might be all over by lunch time."

"I wouldn't go to prison?"

"Well, I can't be absolutely certain of that. They will still think very dimly of a theft from a charity, but if we can come up with some good mitigation, you might get community service; perhaps working for a charity!"

"Even though I'm on a bender?"

"Ah, I didn't know that. What was that for?"

"Theft of a baby's pram from outside a shop in Ermeford."

Why was nothing straightforward where Lee was concerned? Frank wondered.

"I hope there was no baby in it?"

"Ha ha! Good one. No, there wasn't. I got three months suspended for two years."

"How long ago?"

"Last month."

Both for a moment were lost for words.

"So I think I'll go not guilty."

Against his better judgement, Frank did not push the issue further.

"OK, I had better tell the court and the prosecutor."

He wandered off to find out who was prosecuting.

"Ms Williams, I think," reported Ioain. "At least, she's the only CPS lawyer I've seen this morning."

Frank had opposed Jane Williams in the case of the Penwith Pig Rustler and had found her vague and timid. However, as with Frank, that had been one of her very first cases, and rumour had it she was now a more formidable proposition altogether. Unlike Frank, who dealt with a wide range of civil, criminal and family matters, a CPS prosecutor did nothing but prosecute criminal cases, and those with the right forensic mind and sufficient self-confidence could improve very quickly. Her reputation now was that she took no prisoners.

He found her already in court, chatting to Mrs Mills the court clerk as if they were old friends.

Dispensing with any formal greeting, she piled straight in.

"Are you for the defendant?"

"I am."

"I assume the little toerag is pleading guilty?"

Frank wondered if he should take issue with her description of his client though he had to concede that the general public would probably share her view.

"Well, no actually. He's pleading not guilty."

"You're joking. On what basis?"

"No intention to permanently deprive."

"You can't be serious; based on your advice or was it his own idea?"

"That's between me and my client."

"You'll be telling me next that he's electing jury trial."

As an offence of dishonesty, a defendant had the right to choose trial in either the magistrates' court or the Crown Court before a jury. Frank knew that if this highly dubious defence had any chance of success it needed to be aired before a jury of twelve laymen and women rather than before a panel of cynical police-respecting magistrates. Rather selfishly, it had also occurred to him that before a Crown Court, Lee's defence would be presented by a barrister and not himself. He would seek out some world-weary Crown Court "hack", as Horace Rumpole would have put it, who, unabashed by the transparent flimsiness of the argument, would deliver it with flamboyant gusto. Not having to present it himself would be a great relief.

"So, presumably today we can adjourn with a remand on bail for a committal hearing?" asked Frank.

The clerk now opened the court diary.

"How about three weeks today?"

"OK by me," said Frank.

They both looked at the prosecutor.

"I just need a word with the officer in the case – Sergeant Crooke." Frank now noticed for the first time a slim, fit-looking man, immaculately dressed (far too elegantly for a solicitor), sitting at the back of the court. The sergeant and Ms Williams now joined in an intense huddle. A few moments of frenzied whispering followed with several glances by both in Frank's direction. He developed a distinct and uneasy feeling that they were about to spring something unexpected on him.

"Right," said the prosecutor as she rejoined them. "We are opposing bail."

"Why?" Frank almost stammered. "This is a case of theft of a box of no value with a few pounds in it. It's been recovered. It's a not guilty plea. What possible grounds can there be to remand in custody?"

"It's not any old box, it's a charity collection box. We will be calling evidence that it had far more in it when it was taken than when it was recovered. The evidence against him is strong and, most significantly, even though he is only nineteen, he has already amassed twenty-seven previous convictions, the vast majority of which are for theft; and if any more is needed, he is on a bender imposed only last month. Your client is a menace to society. He deserves a custodial sentence and there is a real risk of his absconding."

Frank realised that he should have seen this coming. He also realised that his opponent, who now seemed out of breath after her lengthy diatribe, was not the pushover she had been the previous winter in the Penwith magistrates' court. He had a formidable task before him if Lee was to re-emerge into the light of this beautiful spring day when the hearing was done.

"Right, I had better take instructions," he said, slightly stunned.

"Fifteen minutes," called the clerk after him as he disappeared out of the back of the court.

To his relief, he walked straight into his boss Alan Bradshaw.

"Am I glad to see you," he said. "Have you got a minute?"

"Sure. I'm not on until after you."

Alan Bradshaw was one of the senior partners in Frank's firm with thirty years' experience in criminal law, originally in Yorkshire and for the last twenty years in Cornwall. He was something of a minor legend among the criminal classes of the two counties. He had dropped Frank in it on a couple of occasions by foisting hearings on him at very short notice when Alan had been double booked, but made up for it by inviting Frank along to hearings he was conducting in the Plymouth area. There he could watch the master at work – although Alan himself, modest as always, would never have put it that way. Frank could appreciate the effectiveness of his quietly humorous advocacy style and his ability to give the impression that he was not on anyone's side. He was merely putting forward the obvious and reasonable solution. Magistrates in general did not like aggressive advocates. They liked advocates like Alan. They felt they could trust him, that he was on their side: the side of reason and justice.

Frank quickly outlined his problem.

"Who is your client?" Alan asked. "It wouldn't be Lee by any chance?"

"How did you know?"

"I have represented him before and one of his brothers. It's exactly his sort of modus operandi, and anyway," he admitted slightly sheepishly, "I might be responsible for putting the 'no intention to permanently deprive' defence into his mind when I last represented him. He was moving a pram to a safe place because he thought it was lost!"

"Did that work?"

"No. I agree that in isolation it's a minor offence. Even

with his antecedents you might have had a chance. But with the suspended sentence, you'll be very lucky to avoid a custodial.

"Your only chance," he said as something of an afterthought, "is to suggest a condition that he reports to a local police station daily and then back in court next week for a review. If he sticks with the condition – and it's almost impossible to get him to stick with anything – then he might get a longer bail remand with less stringent conditions next week. Normally, they would want him to surrender his passport – if he has one."

"OK, thanks, Alan. I'll tell him that and I'll tell him you said it's the only way he'll get bail. He'll believe it if it comes from you."

Back in the interview room, Frank brought the bad news.

"The prosecution want you remanded in custody so we will need to make a contested bail application."

Lee's normal good humour seemed unaffected by the news.

"That must be because of the bender."

"That's right. I am not sure if you have heard of my colleague Alan Bradshaw?"

"Everyone's heard of Alan Bradshaw – we know he's a top brief in our family."

"Good, well, I've just bumped into him outside and he thinks we might be struggling a bit on bail because of the suspended sentence. What he recommends is that you offer to present yourself at the local police station on a daily basis until we are next in court to reassure the police that you haven't done a runner."

Frank had expected resistance to this, but again his client was entirely unfazed.

"OK, no problem – I always look forward to spending some time with the coppers."

"And who will you be living with?"

"My parents, as always."

Normally, this would have helped matters, but on this occasion it was best brushed over. The police would be well acquainted with Lee's parents.

"Do you have a passport?"

"What difference does that make?"

"Well, if you have, they will want you to surrender it so that you can't abscond abroad."

"No, I don't, and I've never been abroad and I ain't gonna take up jet-setting any time soon."

"Good, and finally, they are going to bring up your substantial amount of previous. You must have been bailed before?"

"Yep."

"And have you always turned up in court when you have been bailed?"

"Yep."

"And everything you have told me is true? I don't want any surprises in court."

Was there a moment's hesitation? Frank wasn't sure.

"The last person I would lie to is my brief," beamed Lee.

"Right then, good, I'll tell them we're ready."

They were called straight in and the formalities quickly dispensed with. It was agreed that the case would come back to court the following Wednesday. Frank then stood up and made his application for a remand on bail.

"Does the prosecutor object to bail?" asked the court clerk.

"We certainly do," replied Ms Williams forcefully.

"Your grounds?"

"The nature of the offence – this was the theft of a charity collection box; the defendant's antecedents – despite his tender years he has already amassed twenty-seven convictions, mostly for offences of a similar nature. Furthermore, the evidence against the defendant is strong. There are two identification witnesses and when he was apprehended by the police, some thirty minutes later, he was still in possession of the box and some of its contents. If this is not enough, he is already subject to a suspended sentence committed only a matter of weeks ago. As such, he is at serious risk of a prison sentence both for this offence and for breach of a suspended sentence and there is a real risk that he will abscond."

"Thank you, Ms Williams," said the clerk. "Mr Gilbert, do you want the officer in the case to give evidence?"

"Yes please, I do have a few questions."

Sergeant Crooke was sworn.

Frank began his examination with trepidation, hoping that Lee had had the good sense not to lie to his own advocate.

"Sergeant Crooke, the prosecuting solicitor has told the court that the defendant has a large number of convictions."

"Yes – twenty-seven."

"Would it be true to say that taken individually, they were all to the lower end of the scale of possible theft offences?"

"Yes, I suppose so – but there are an awful lot of them."

"And, would it also be true to say that none of them involved violence?"

"Yes, I think so."

"And for how many of those offences was the defendant remanded on bail to appear in court?"

"Well, most of them, probably."

Frank knew that everything could depend on the answer to the next question.

"And how often did he fail to appear?"

"Ah, never, as far as I am aware."

Well, that was a relief.

"So, if he has always honoured his bail obligations in the past, why do you think he will fail to do so now?"

Frank knew the answer to this before he had finished asking.

"He wasn't in breach of a suspended sentence then."

"But we don't know if he is now – he is innocent until convicted."

The sergeant's response to that was something of a guffaw.

Frank now addressed the court.

"Your Worships, the defendant has never breached bail previously and if the police are seriously concerned that he will do so now, he is willing to attend each morning between now and the next hearing at Ermeford Police Station. He has a settled place of residence where he has lived all his life" – did the good sergeant guffaw again? – "he tells me he has never been abroad and has no passport. As the next hearing is only five days away, I would submit that there is little likelihood of his absconding and that it is reasonable to grant bail on those terms."

The magistrates conferred briefly and the chairperson then responded.

"Mr Gilbert, can we briefly hear your client confirm what you have just told us in the witness box?"

"Of course, Your Worships."

Lee took the oath without needing to refer to the card.

"Mr Facey," asked Frank, "can you please tell the court your address?"

He did so, giving an address in one of north Plymouth's largest council estates.

"And how long have you lived there?"

"Always."

"And who else lives there?"

"My mum and dad, Wayne, my brother, and my little sister."

"Do you hold a passport?"

"No, I ain't got one."

"And you have heard me tell the court that you are willing to turn up at the Ermeford police station every morning until we are back in court next Wednesday?"

"Yep."

"And do you confirm you will do that?"

"Yep."

"And you understand that if you don't do that and sign in with the desk officer there, you will be in breach of your bail conditions and liable to be arrested?"

"Yep, I know that. I've done it before."

"Do Your Worships have any questions?" Frank asked the bench.

"Just one or two," replied the chairperson. "Mr Facey, you say you don't have a passport, have you ever had one?"

"Nope, never."

"Your solicitor has quite properly asked you to confirm that if bail is granted and you do not comply with the conditions you understand that you will be liable to arrest. Can I add that you would then be brought back before the court and would run the very real risk of spending the entire period until your trial in custody and that might be for many weeks. Even if you are then acquitted for this offence, breach of bail is itself a criminal offence, and as you are already subject to a suspended sentence, you would be sentenced for both breaches. Do you understand?"

"Yes, sir, I understand."

The chairperson conferred briefly with his colleagues.

"Right then, the defendant is remanded on bail to appear at this court next Wednesday morning, subject to the condition that he attends each morning until then at Ermeford Police Station at 10 am to answer bail commencing tomorrow morning."

The bench rose; the hearing was a success. Why, therefore, did Frank feel so apprehensive? The court had stressed in no uncertain terms the consequences of non-compliance, but he still felt he needed another go.

"So, Lee, where will you be at 10 am tomorrow morning and the next four mornings after that?"

"At Ermeford Police Station, of course. Don't worry, Mr Gilbert, you can rely on me," Lee replied airily.

"And you have to sign in with the desk officer and he needs to sign too – and bring some ID."

"My passport?"

Frank fixed him with a dark stare.

"Ha ha! You worry too much. I don't have one. I'll take my birth certificate."

"Good. Either Mr Bradshaw or I will meet you here at 9.30 am on Wednesday morning, when you can enter a plea and decide whether to be tried in this court or the Crown Court."

They said their goodbyes and Frank left court feeling he

had done what he could, but still afflicted by an inexplicable feeling of foreboding.

The ferry to Roscoff, France, set sail at 11 pm that evening. The fair weather of the morning was a distant memory and, even at its mooring, the huge passenger ferry was already rolling ominously. Frank did not suffer unduly with sea sickness – or *mal de mer* since he was going to France – but he was the designated driver for the following day, when they would journey over the moorland and past the lakes of central Brittany to the medieval walled city of Concarneau on the south Breton coast. Frank knew he could not live with Vic or George in the drinking stakes. He knew they would hit the bar at the first opportunity. Wisely, he ensconced himself in his cabin for the first hour. Dick, however, would need rescuing. He would try to match his fellow drinkers without their vast capacity and, in the absence of Frank's steadying hand, would soon be beyond redemption. Frank knew his appearance at the bar could not be further delayed.

He could hear the hubbub from the bar before he reached it. The large room was heaving and the assembled drinkers, as if forming one mass of humanity, rocked back and forth with the rolling of the boat. From the far distance, Vic's unmistakable rich cockney drifted across the drinking hall.

"We few, we 'appy few, we band of brothers." Ah, thought Frank, the Agincourt scene. This scene from *Henry V* performed by Dick and Vic was a minor sensation in their little world of Plymouth business folk. It had been performed in pubs, restaurants and other social gatherings throughout the city of Plymouth and its environs. Dick would start it off with his impeccable "Gieldgudian" delivery. Vic would follow on in vibrant cockney with its dropped aitches and elongated East End vowels.

Both knew the scene verbatim. Dick could imitate the action of a tiger as well as any thespian. Vic would strip his sleeve and show the scars he had upon St Crispin's Day with admirable dramatic vigour.

Sometimes it was received with dismissive disdain, but mostly the initially bemused audiences would warm to it, intrigued by the unique nature of the rendition. The passengers on a Friday night ferry to France, whether British or French, were the right kind of audience. The well-oiled drinkers cheered them on and joined in with the bits they recognised.

Frank knew he would get dragged in if he joined them. He had seen it so many times he knew most of the words. So he sidled up to the bar and put in an order for a pint of Carlsberg Export. The drink took an age to arrive and, when it eventually did, and Frank flourished his wad of Francs to the barman, to his surprise the barman declined to accept.

"Already paid for," he announced.

"Really, who by?"

The barman pointed vaguely in the direction of a large and rowdy group. A young man was beaming and waving enthusiastically in his direction.

"This story shall the good man teach his son," he heard drifting across the throng followed by, "That's my brief!" from a familiar voice.

"I wouldn't be here without him!"

Frank's lawyer's logic defied the evidence of his senses. Lee could not be here. He was in Plymouth contemplating the error of his ways and an early morning visit to the police station, not living it up with his mates on a cross-channel ferry.

"From this day to the ending of the world
But we in it shall be remembered."

The boat lurched violently, throwing Frank against the bar just as he was attempting his first swig. As he righted himself, an arm draped itself around his shoulder and his worst fears were realised.

"Mr Gilbert, I wouldn't be here without you."

As if to acknowledge Frank's success, a huge cheer erupted across the crowded room as Vic concluded his eulogy of those who fought with their king upon St Crispin's Day.

"You shouldn't be here at all. We promised the court you would answer bail tomorrow morning."

"Don't worry. They won't miss me for one day. I'll surrender myself on Sunday morning."

"No, you won't. This ferry comes back on Monday. They'll issue a warrant for your arrest with no chance of bail."

"Well, perhaps I won't come back then."

Seeing the horrified look on Frank's face, Lee quickly withdrew this.

"Only joking. I'll go straight to the nearest police station as soon as we get back. But it's my brother Wayne's twenty-first birthday trip. I couldn't miss it."

"And another thing, I cannot accept this drink from you." Frank noticed he had either drunk or spilled most of it already.

"Why not? Do you want something else?"

"No, I can't be seen with you. I would be condoning your presence here."

"You wot?"

Frank glanced furtively around. Was that slim female about to down a large glass of bubbly Ms Williams, the CPS prosecutor? Was the well-dressed, middle-aged man leaning on the bar a few drinkers along Sergeant Crooke? To his relief, the only familiar face was Vic's, his balding dome radiantly unmistakable as he fought through the crowd towards him.

"Come on, Sir Humphrey, we need you for 'The Owl and the Pussy-Cat'. Dick says I'm too common for the elegant fowl so he needs you. I'm only fit for the piggy-wig."

What a good evening this could have been, Frank pondered ruefully. Now his only thought was to tactfully put as much distance between himself and his unwelcome absconding client.

"I'll be right there," he lied. "Can I introduce you to my client Lee? Lee, this is Vic, Vic this is Lee. Lee and Dick already know each other. Lee will make an excellent owl. He's a quick learner and a great actor."

Lee looked bemused and slightly alarmed as Vic's brawny ex-stoker's arm whisked him off through the jovial drinkers. If he felt some embarrassment at being press-ganged into a leading role in an impromptu public performance of "The Owl and the Pussy-Cat" before an audience of his fellow petty criminals at their most boisterously satirical then that was no more than he deserved.

Mournfully, Frank slunk away to his cabin.

POSTSCRIPT

As soon as Frank arrived in the office on Tuesday morning, he rang Alan Bradshaw and related to him the whole sorry tale. They agreed that Frank was compromised and Alan should represent Lee in court on the following day.

At the hearing, Lee was remanded in custody until the trial. The issue of the joint presence of Lee and his former solicitor on the same cross-channel ferry the previous Friday evening did not come before the court.

Five weeks later, Alan Bradshaw again represented Lee before the Dartbridge magistrates. At the hearing, Lee pleaded guilty to breach of bail conditions and theft of the charity box. He admitted breach of his suspended sentence. He was sentenced to three months' imprisonment for the theft and two further three-month sentences for breach of the bail condition and breach of the suspended sentence, the latter two terms to run concurrently. Eight months later, Lee instructed Frank to represent him on a charge of theft of a vintage copy of the *Complete Works of Shakespeare* from an antiquarian bookshop on Plymouth Barbican.

Part Four

The Case of the Forged Signature

"Mr Ronnie Best and Mr Glen Terrell are here for you, Mr Gilbert."

"Thanks, Debs – send them through."

Ronnie Best was an operator of a slightly different kind to the usual eccentrics and down-and-outs Frank represented. Not only was he somewhat more competent, but also his aspirations were higher. Medium-scale frauds, and occasional forays into the world of drugs and tobacco smuggling, were more in his line. This of course could mean that, if convicted, he would be at risk of a greater prison sentence than the two or three months most of Frank's clients could expect. Indeed he had already served two sentences of twelve and thirty months; the first for VAT fraud and the second for hiring a superannuated fishing boat and sailing it back across the channel full of drugs.

The drug-smuggling sentence would have looked rather lenient but for the general incompetence of the operation. The boat had been unseaworthy, had sprung a leak and the cargo, which was unloaded by the police who had got wind of the operation and were awaiting the smugglers in a remote South Devon cove, was entirely waterlogged. After his release, the drug squad kept a close eye on him as they suspected his involvement in other similar trips with more successful outcomes.

Thereafter, despite occasional encouragement from old friends from his East End days, Ronnie had declared himself retired from his youthful follies and ready to devote himself to more sophisticated and legal "business ventures".

Ronnie was an extremely plausible fellow – articulate and intelligent, witty and amiable. A man with such charisma and acumen had no need to expose himself to the risks of illegal, night-time smuggling trips. So, in prison, he had taken advantage of the captive audience and set up a business consultancy and mortgage brokerage.

Many of his fellow inmates had aspirations as entrepreneurs on their release. They aspired to be bar owners, publicans, operators of small-time security companies, even landlords of residential properties. In most cases though, their understanding of how to go about setting up such an operation was non-existent. However, that did not matter as they had the good fortune to be doing their time in the company of Ronnie Best: entrepreneur supreme. Whatever they wanted to know, he could tell them; introductions could be made; finance could be arranged; consultations could take place in the prison canteen. Fees were modest at this stage – cigarettes, general sharing of prison rations. Ronnie's time and expenditure could be properly remunerated when they were released and the business he had helped set up began to thrive. Ronnie was in such demand that even some of the wardens sought his advice, and that sort of advice could be paid for now. Ronnie existed in some luxury, excused from prison duties and with access to benefits such as alcohol, which he could enjoy himself, dispense to his clients or sell on to other prisoners.

And now he was free, just as a new source of easy money was released upon the world; obtaining residential mortgages for clients considered by the financial services industry to be commercial customers, or as Frank would have described it, "mortgage fraud".

A mortgage lender could have no idea when it received a mortgage application on a residential property whether the applicant intended to live in it or let it. Unless the property was let at the time of the mortgage valuation, the lender's valuer could also have no idea. The lender was entirely reliant on the honesty of the applicant and the broker in declaring the true proposed use on the application form. In the 1980s, mortgages for property letting were hard to come by. The modern buy-to-let mortgage did not exist but the demand for them was no less great than in later years. Most legitimate mortgages for rented properties came from banks. They were treated as commercial finance. The interest rates were high and the percentage of the valuation available from the lender was low: 60–70% of the valuation as a maximum.

Residential mortgages on the borrower's home, however, were much more freely available – in some cases laughably so. The City and Village Building Society, for example, would lend 100% of the purchase price at a minimal interest rate and allow borrowers to self-certify their income. A broker who could satisfy the huge demand for finance on rented properties by arranging mortgages on residential terms could make a fortune. Ronnie had learnt this from an ancient former mortgage broker he had met inside, who was serving a three-year stretch for providing forged employers' salary details to mortgage lenders. In the age of self-certification, as Ronnie was aware, this was a risk he would not need to run.

He had arranged a particularly dodgy mortgage for himself to fund the purchase of the Captain Flint, an immensely popular public house in Devonport, the old naval area of Plymouth, well known for its flexible drinking hours and seedy entertainment. The pub was a gold mine and operated alongside his lucrative brokerage business, dispensing mortgage offers on rented properties like confetti and receiving payment from all parties involved. He could pocket an introductory commission from the lender, a commission on the supporting life assurance, an arrangement fee from the borrower, which Ronnie could often persuade the lender to add to the loan, and, in some cases, an introductory backhander from the solicitor handling the legal work.

Word got around quickly amongst buyers and estate agents that Ronnie was the man who could facilitate the transactions and allow virtually penniless buyers to become landlords. The punters would flock "lemming-like" to his palatial office behind the bar of the Captain Flint. There, surrounded by busts of Drake, Raleigh and other mementos of Plymouth's glory days as the maritime capital of England, he would accept, godfather-like, their up-front payment, in wads of cash only, towards his fee. He would assure them that an immensely affordable and perfectly legitimate mortgage for the whole of the purchase price, with all their fees thrown in, was theirs for the asking.

"You may not know Glen, but you know *of* him," Ronnie began.

"He was the man in the Charles Cross cells on our opening night, when you and the delightful Nell were nearly lost at sea in your mate's boat."

"I remember it well," said Frank, smiling.

Ronnie had recently opened a plush new bar and restaurant on Plymouth's Barbican, a posher affair by far than his existing operation at the Captain Flint. He had given it a much more exotic name, "Nombre de Dios", after the bay in the Caribbean where Plymouth's most famous son Sir Francis Drake had died and been buried at sea. Frank had received an invitation for himself plus friends and had invited Nell, a paralegal from Hollingberry & Co, a sole practitioner firm just around the corner from Frank's office, to accompany him.

A few days before the opening, his old school friend Alec had announced that his "DIY" service on his trusty old cabin cruiser "Norman" was complete and that the vessel was seaworthy. Did Frank fancy a trip across Plymouth Sound to Cawsand Bay and back? Frank was not sure that he did. Alec, on the face of it, had no marine engineering skills. He was a Barbican gift shop proprietor and part-time VAT consultant and author. The cheery insouciance with which he embarked upon maintenance to his boat's engine was unnerving to such an inveterate worrier as Frank. He wondered whether he could use the opening invitation as an excuse, but they had been enthusiastically contemplating the relaunch of the redoubtable Norman for months. He could not let his friend down.

So he rang Nell and asked if they could meet slightly later.

"Why, have you found something better to do?"

"Not really. I've been invited out on my friend's boat and I can't really let him down. He's very excited about the relaunch."

"Isn't there room for three?"

Frank had no doubt that Alec would be only too pleased to show off his nautical skills to an attractive young woman, but before agreeing he owed it to her to explain the risks.

"I should warn you that Alec has a bit of form where breaking down at sea and running aground is concerned, and he has carried out his engine service himself."

"What's the problem – you can swim, can't you?"

"It's you I'm worried about."

"I can swim, I'm very good at it. I'll bring my swimsuit!"

So it was settled then, and on the evening of Ronnie's opening party, Frank, Nell and Alec were chugging across the Sound towards Cawsand Bay and into a growing storm coming out of the Channel from the south-west. Lowering black clouds banked up over Rame Head and the sea began to roll. Their plan had been to drop anchor in Cawsand Bay and enjoy a bottle of wine and pastries provided by Nell.

"That looks ominous," said Alec. "We'd better turn around and head back. We need to get inside the breakwater before that hits."

They turned in the bay and had found the protection of the nineteenth-century granite and limestone sea wall before the swell heaved and the heavens opened. The old timbers of the cabin cruiser's hull began to creak and groan. As the vessel bounced across the roaring sea, waves crashed over its prow. By the time they regained the protection of Sutton Harbour, the wind had attained gale force and all three were drenched with brine and freezing. Fortunately, the restored Elizabethan warehouse for which they were heading, and the good hot food and cosy hospitality it promised, were only a few steps from the harbour. Alec had the look of a salty sea dog at the best of times, and when he cast open the large wooden double doors, windswept and bedraggled, and strode into the crowded bar, he was greeted with a hush of nervous anticipation. Rising to the occasion, he bellowed forth the words of a popular TV advert of the time: "I ain't never seen a night like it."

The more familiar and less intimidating faces of Nell and Frank loomed up behind him and the assembled revellers relaxed.

"Frankie, you've made it – but only just by the looks of it," came Ronnie's unmistakable voice from the midst of a crowd of drinkers at the bar.

"What can I get you and who's your beautiful friend? I don't mean this fellow." He gesticulated pleasantly at Alec.

"This is my friend Nell and this is Alec, who has just skippered us back across the Sound from Cawsand in this hurricane."

"Jesus! Across the Sound, you look like you've been in it – better check the weather next time. Anyway, drinks are on the house. Come and meet my friends."

Frank briefly scanned Ronnie's various friends. He recognised a few of them; they were the type regularly in need of lawyers. Notwithstanding, they were an affluent crowd and normally Frank would have welcomed the introduction, but not tonight. The three of them slipped away into a cosy nook, near one of the various open fires, to warm up and dry off.

Frank glanced guiltily at Nell. If possible she looked even more drenched than Alec, who, as skipper, had insisted on standing at the helm defying the angry sea. He hoped that she didn't feel uncomfortable in the presence of so many women dressed to kill, with her soaking hair and mascara running down her cheeks. The look quite suited her, he thought, with her dark colouring and titian hair. For him, she was still the most attractive woman in the room.

"Well, I'm sorry about that," he said sheepishly. "I was looking forward to a gentle cruise across the Sound."

"No need to apologise. It's the most exciting first date I've ever had."

He liked this girl. Hopefully her reference to a first date meant that there might be a second.

Ronnie now arrived with a bottle of Italian white and two pints of real ale. In his wake came a waitress bearing a huge platter of seafood and a large basket of hot, freshly baked bread. Another followed with three warm towels; Ronnie really knew how to dispense hospitality.

"Tuck in – all on the house. But afterwards can I have a professional word with you, Frank?"

"Sure, fire away now if it's not too confidential."

"OK, well, sorry to ruin your evening but do you know my mate Glen Terrell?"

"I don't think I do."

"Well, he's a good chap but too much of a ladies' man for some. He should have been with us this evening but I've just had a frantic call from his girlfriend Chantelle. He's been arrested, he's in Charles Cross and they're not intending to interview him until the morning."

"What's he accused of?"

"Forgery – forging a deed for the sale of a hotel. He usually instructs Harry Paget but he's abroad on holiday. But they can't keep him overnight, can they? He's claustrophobic; he's desperate to get out."

"The problem with more complex cases like forgery is that they will want the investigating officer to conduct the interview – and that's likely to be a detective inspector or a detective sergeant, who may not be available straight away. But if he doesn't have any relevant previous or hasn't jumped bail before then we might be able to get him out if I speak to the desk sergeant. No guarantees though, and I'm probably going to have to go up there."

"OK. I'll ring Chantelle and ask about the previous. It would be great if you could go up. He'll make it worth your while, or I will, if he doesn't."

"OK. Well, I'd better not drink any more of this then."

"And while you're away, I'll look after Nell," said Ronnie, smiling paternally in her direction.

Frank did not like the sound of this.

"No need," she responded quickly. "I work in the law too. I will go to the police station as Frank's assistant – his clerk."

"That's settled then," said Frank. "Now, let's tuck into this food before Alec eats it all."

Ronnie disappeared but was back a few minutes later.

"I've spoken to Chantelle and she doesn't think he's been in trouble with the police before. She says if you can't come up straight away can you ring the desk sergeant, Sergeant Wise? Glen's desperate to get out tonight."

"I can go up now but I think I'll ring the desk sergeant anyway to let him know I'm coming. Do you have a phone I can use, Ronnie?"

"Sure, come with me."

"No need," interjected Alec with a look of quiet triumphalism.

He rummaged in his bag and brought out a huge black brick of an object with a single antenna.

"No need for defensive weaponry in my establishments," said Ronnie.

"It's a mobile phone," said Nell.

"Absolutely right," agreed Alec, who was something of an early adopter in these areas.

"No need to leave your seat. Just give me the good sergeant's number and I'll put you right through."

The station number was produced and Alex extended the aerial and dialled it. Nothing happened. Alec looked crestfallen. After a moment he perked up.

"Must be the reception; thick walls in these old Elizabethan buildings. Let's go outside."

"Have you forgotten that the mother of all storms is blowing out there?"

"No worries, chaps," said Ronnie. "I'll take you to the gents. They're in a modern annex – much better reception."

Sure enough, the strange device worked perfectly there and in no time, for reasons of confidentiality and his technological incompetence, Frank was standing in a locked cubicle with Alec, with the mobile phone weighing as much as a respectably weighted dumb-bell, attached to his ear and in deep conversation with the desk sergeant.

To his surprise, the sergeant was more than willing to consider an overnight release.

"It's not his fault we can't interview him tonight. Subject to one thing, and if he leaves his passport with us and undertakes to be back here tomorrow at 2 pm for interview with Inspector Jennings, then I'm happy to grant police bail."

"Great, thanks, and what's the one thing?"

"We want to know where he is staying tonight. The young floozy who's been here all evening has given us her address but now another lady has turned up, a much more respectable-looking lady who claims to be his wife and who seems to think he's going home with her. She turned up when the first lady, Chantelle, was in the loo and neither of them seem to know each other. They are both sitting in the foyer ignoring one another and I suppose they both think they're waiting for different people. I wouldn't like to be in your client's shoes when they find out they're not."

Sergeant Wise could not disguise his amusement.

"Right," said Frank. "Have you told him there are two women waiting for him?"

"Not yet," he replied gleefully. "I'm just about to. Even the job of a humble desk sergeant has to have some perks."

Sorting out this difficulty seemed to be outside of Frank's remit.

"OK, well, if you're releasing him I won't bother to come up, but if either of you wants to speak to me can you ring me on this number?"

"Will do."

Back in the bar, Frank relayed this mixed news to the others. Ronnie looked appalled.

"Margot has turned up? How did she know he was there? My God, he's in trouble now."

"Does he still live with his wife?" asked Frank.

"Well, yes, sort of, most of the time. Margot is a fine woman. She has put up with Glen's philandering for years, chucked him out a few times but always taken him back when he swore he would change his ways. And through it all, she has single-handedly run their successful hotel business so that he can blow the profits on gambling, wining and dining loose women, and running his beloved E-Type.

"You'll notice I'm a great supporter of Margot – wonderful woman, quite attractive too. But she wouldn't be so complimentary about me. She thinks I'm the 'eminence grise' – is that what you call it? – behind all his bad behaviour. Without me, the deluded woman thinks Glen would be a fine and faithful husband, but take it from me, he wouldn't; he needs no encouragement. With my irresistible charms," he said, winking at Nell, who ignored him, "I can concentrate on the really attractive ones. Glen, on the other hand, will shack up with anyone who'll have him."

Frank glanced at Nell – was that a look of amusement or contempt? He couldn't quite tell.

"So, what's his relationship with Chantelle?" she asked suddenly.

"A long time on-and-off girlfriend. Margot knows of several of his affairs, but Chantelle has been more serious and he has tried hard to keep her a secret."

At that moment, the sound of Straus's "The Blue Danube" inexplicably started up from somewhere near.

"Ah! Someone's calling," exclaimed Alec triumphantly. He pressed a button on his brick and recited the number into it.

"Sergeant Wise for you." He passed the phone to Frank.

"This shift gets better and better," chuckled the sergeant as if speaking from a world away. "I have never seen a man in more abject terror. I told him that his good lady wife was here to take him home. I offered to introduce her to his friend Chantelle. I think he would have confessed on the

79

spot to anything we accused him of. He pleaded with me to let him stay in our nice comfortable cell overnight and to tell his wife that we were refusing bail until his interview. He begged me to find some way of telling the two ladies separately so that they don't realise they're both waiting for the same man."

"That sounds like a problem for you."

"Not at all. I'm a kind-hearted chap and your client has given me a great deal of amusement this evening. I can't wait to tell my colleagues. So I went out and called them both into separate interview rooms using only their Christian names and explained that forgery was a serious offence and we couldn't let him out until after his interview tomorrow. Chantelle shed a few tears and Mrs Terrell left muttering angrily about abuse of power and a police state."

"OK, thanks for letting me know. I think his usual solicitor will represent him from now on."

Frank handed back the phone. He could sense his companions' interest and Ronnie shuffled forward expectantly.

"You're never going to believe this. He wants to stay in the cells. He's more afraid of his wife than he is of enclosed spaces."

Ronnie let rip an immense, raucous belly laugh.

"You wimp, Glenny!"

...

And now, six months later, the man himself was sitting in his office seeking his advice.

Ronnie continued his introductory account.

"Glen stayed in the cells overnight, as you know, and he was interviewed by Inspector Jennings the next day for suspected forgery. He has now been charged with that and Harry Paget is representing him and the case is going to the Crown Court, but Harry doesn't do civil work. That's why we're here."

"So, how is this now a civil matter? And I hope you won't mind, Ronnie, and thanks very much for your intro and summary, but perhaps Glen ought to answer this. Is it OK to call you Glen?"

"No problem. Well, it's like this, the documents I'm supposed to have forged are the contract and transfer deed for the sale of our hotel on The Hoe – The Armada."

"Is this the one you ran with your wife? Was it jointly owned?"

"Yes, we owned it together. Our marriage was not going well and we agreed to sell it. We had it valued and put it on the market with McCormacks, the commercial agents. We received several offers, not as much as we wanted, but we agreed to accept the higher one after the agent had checked that the buyer had the money. I even agreed that Margot could have 60% of the sale proceeds to persuade her to accept the deal as her matrimonial solicitor had advised her she was entitled to more than half – I had no idea why. Apparently I would have a higher earning capacity after we separated. Once again, I have no idea why. She is a qualified teacher, though she never worked as one. I'm not qualified to do anything."

"Right, Glen." Frank thought Glen was wandering and he ought to take control. "Do you have solicitors advising you in the matrimonial matter?"

"Yes. If you agree to act for me I will be paying for four different firms of lawyers. I'm using Hammonds in the divorce, but they're far too expensive for the conveyancing. So Ronnie kindly recommended a friend of his who is much cheaper."

"Who's that?"

"Mike Roberts."

Frank did not comment. He knew of Mike Roberts as the one-man band who, rumour had it, lubricated the legal wheels of Ronnie's dodgy mortgage cases.

"So presumably Hammonds agreed that apportionment with your wife's solicitors?"

"Yes, and everything was going fine, but at the last minute the bitch changed her mind and demanded more. But it was too late."

"Why?"

"'Cos she'd already signed the papers."

"So, did she change her mind after contracts for the sale had been exchanged?"

"No – yes – well, she says she changed her mind before."

"When did she tell Mr Roberts, who presumably was acting for both of you in the sale?"

"She says she wrote to him before exchange of contracts. We were due to exchange contracts and complete on the same day."

"So, I'm confused. How did exchange and completion take place?"

"She had already signed the documents and Mike didn't receive her letter until afterwards."

"So what's the problem then?"

"Well, the bloody woman is now saying that she never signed any documents. She is saying that I signed her name on them."

"And did you?"

"Of course not."

"Did Mr Roberts send her the documents direct or via her solicitor?"

"No, neither."

"How did she get them then?"

"He gave them to me to get her to sign."

Frank's heart sank. How could he move this forward without criticising a fellow professional, albeit a seemingly suspect one?

"That doesn't really help. The Law Society advises against that course," he said, by way of understatement.

The next question was an obvious one.

"Who witnessed your wife's signature?"

"Our mate Bob."

"Whose mate? Yours or your wife's?"

"Mine and Ronnie's, and he works for Ronnie."

This did not help matters either.

"So, the next question I imagine the police will ask, if they haven't already, is where and when did your wife and Bob meet for him to witness her signature?"

Glen's hesitation was perceptible. Ronnie came to his aid.

"He called around at Margot's place a few days later, didn't he, Glen?"

"Yes, he did. We arranged it for her so she wouldn't have to find a witness."

"So Bob would give evidence that Margot signed it?"

"Yes, I suppose so. If you think that is necessary?"

"He's going to have to if she persists in denying that she signed it.

"But why do you need my help?" Frank continued. "You

already have Harry Paget representing you and in criminal matters in this part of the world they don't come much better than Harry."

"Harry's fine but he only does criminal work. He can't help with what's happened now."

"You mean there's more?"

"You don't know the half of it," said Ronnie wryly.

"I'm all ears."

"When Margot found that the completion date had gone through, her solicitors applied to the court for an order to freeze the transaction."

"I would have to research that, but my initial view is that they might have problems getting that order as an innocent buyer shouldn't be prejudiced, and your wife's claim should be over the sale proceeds."

"Well, they got it. The hotel is frozen and the buyers aren't pleased."

"OK. Presumably it's what they call an interim injunction and is due back before the court for a full hearing?"

"Yes, it's back again next week and that's why I need your help."

Ronnie interrupted again.

"I think Frank needs to know that Margot claims that Glen, Bob and the buyers are all in it together and he needs to know who the buyers are."

"I was getting to that."

Frank now perceived for the first time that Glen was scared.

"The buyers are the Harveys."

"Ah, I see your problem."

The Harveys were the closest thing Plymouth had to the Krays. Mother Rhoda, father Derek and their two sons, Denny and Des, operated two clubs and a host of bars and betting shops. They also had a virtual monopoly of Plymouth's private security operations.

Father Derek had a variety of convictions as a young man, but for the last thirty years or so had managed to stay clear of the law and, on the face of it, now ran a respectable and highly successful business. The dance-halls-cum-drinking-dens in Plymouth's notorious Union Street, which had hosted brawls between locals and matelots in the post-war naval city and where Derek had begun his career in the hospitality industry, were a thing of the past. Small, seedy establishments still existed in old Union Street for those looking for a fight, but Derek Harvey had grander ideas. He knew where the money was in the new yuppie dawn. He had moved out of Union Street and started afresh. The new Harvey establishments were plush, elegant and priced to discourage the riff-raff. Derek wanted the young professionals – they had money to spend. Any trouble-makers would have Des and Denny's security operation to deal with – no longer bouncers, not even doormen, but security consultants; firm but polite, at least while in the view of potential witnesses or a security camera.

Rhoda's side of the business had similarly gone upmarket. There were few now who had the courage or the stupidity to allude to her formative years as Plymouth's premier Madam. Now her clients were businessmen visiting the city in need of attractive high-class dinner companions. But even this line of business she now felt to be beneath her. Her greatest aspiration was respectability, and for some years she had dreamt of the hotel business – a high-class operation, ideally a four-star on Plymouth Hoe. Recently, she had set her heart on The Armada: three substantial adjoining terraced houses in eighteenth-century John-Foulston style on one of The Hoe's most imposing streets. Derek had promised to do all in his power to make her dreams come true. Ronnie had effected the introduction and a deal was done. The price was £80,000–£100,000 more than it was worth. Derek wasn't going to quibble knowing how much his darling Rhoda wanted it. Hands were shaken on the deal, and once hands were shaken on a deal with the Harveys you didn't back out.

"So," said Ronnie. "You can see why Glen needs to have this freezing order unfrozen at the next hearing."

Frank could certainly see this.

"Were the Harveys represented at the injunction hearing?"

"No," said Glen. "They say it's my job to sort it out. They've honoured their side of the deal so I have to honour mine; which I suppose is true. They place a lot of emphasis on honour. They send their boys Denny and Des round to visit me at home every few evenings to remind me. They are polite enough, but they point out that their parents paid over the odds and they want their hotel."

"Have you met Denny and Des?" asked Ronnie.

"I can't say I've had that pleasure."

"Strapping lads – built like the proverbial, and they employ about thirty others just like themselves."

Frank pondered a moment.

"So if they paid over the odds, why does your wife have a problem with the sale?"

"Several reasons. She says she never realised how much we owed on the property. Over four-hundred grand to the bank, including the overdraft, and another sixty-grand-odd to Tamar Valley Finance Limited, which she claims she knew nothing about."

"Ouch! What was the interest rate on that?"

"24%; no more than the bank overdraft."

"If she didn't know about it, is she claiming you forged that too?"

"Not exactly. She just says she doesn't remember it, but she is adamant I forged her signature on the sale deed."

"Which you have told me you didn't."

"That's right, Bob witnessed her signature."

Did Frank believe this? He wasn't sure, but it wasn't his job to accuse his client of lying if he only suspected but didn't know.

"What about the contract? That's not a deed so it doesn't need witnessing."

"She says I forged that too."

"Which you also deny?"

"Sure."

"But she originally agreed to the sale?"

"Yep, and we agreed a sixty-forty split in her favour – through solicitors. But at the last minute she said she wanted 75%. She thought she had me over a barrel – I couldn't let down the Harveys, but I didn't need to because she had already signed."

"Where are the sale proceeds now? Have they been distributed?"

"No. They are sat in Mike Robert's client account."

"So, how much are we arguing over? 15% of how much?"

"Well, Mike is holding about £320,000 and she wants £240,000 of it; which is outrageous as she is now sitting in our mortgage-free house which she isn't going to give up without a fight."

"Looked at slightly differently, the 15% difference is £48,000. Isn't there some deal you can do with your wife over that which might not resolve the criminal charge but would get you out of your difficulty with the Harveys?"

"Does that mean you think that we will lose at the next hearing?" asked Ronnie.

"Not necessarily. Unless Glen's wife can prove to the court on the balance of probabilities that the Harveys were complicit in a forgery, then they should be viewed as the innocent party."

"First time for everything," beamed Ronnie.

Frank smiled.

"There is a concept in law called bona fide purchaser for value without notice. What this means is that a purchaser of land from the registered owner of that land at the Land Registry should not be bound by any claims against the land which are not disclosed at the Land Registry, unless the purchaser is aware of them. I will need to undertake a bit of research to see if that applies to a forged deed. It may not. If it does, then the Harveys may be treated as the innocent party and get good title to the hotel, leaving you and your wife to argue over the sale proceeds.

"But it may not just be a question of who is right or wrong. You have to consider the commercial realities. Fighting this will cost a lot of money. It might be cheaper to do a deal with your wife than fight it."

"So you don't think I've got a good case?"

"Some old advocate, I forget who, once said that the best case in the world has a 60% chance of success and the worst case has a 40% chance. All litigation is extremely unpredictable and expensive. We will need to instruct a barrister with specialist experience in this area and the whole case could cost several tens of thousands of pounds. The firm will want me to collect about five thousand of that on account and more as we go along."

"Could I be entitled to legal aid?"

"You would need to be financially eligible. You work as a financial adviser?"

"Well, a mortgage broker and endowment salesman really."

"Don't worry about the cost," interjected Ronnie. "I will lend you what you need and we can set the loan off against commissions for buy-to-let cases introduced."

Frank wondered if he should point out that this arrangement could leave Glen forever in Ronnie's thrall, a fly in his labyrinthine web. Such was the enthusiasm of Glen's response that he didn't bother.

"That would be fantastic, mate, if you would."

"OK," Frank said. "Then can I ask you to think about things overnight and if you are still of the same mind, we will need a couple of meetings to take a full statement and I will look for a suitable barrister."

The next day, Frank received a call from Glen confirming he wanted to fight this out in court, and the day after, £5,000 in cash turned up in reception delivered by Ronnie. These were the days before solicitors were obliged to assume that all clients were money launderers and check the source of funds so the money went straight into the firm's client account.

Frank got to work on the case, interviewing Glen and preparing a long witness statement of his evidence. He would also need to meet with Bob to take a statement confirming that he witnessed the crucial signature. He suspected he might need to resist pressure from Ronnie to be present at that meeting. There was little point in taking a statement from Bob that he wouldn't confirm in the witness box. Finally and most interestingly, he would need to meet with Mike Roberts. Taking a witness statement from another lawyer, especially when that lawyer's conduct might be called into question in the case, was always a delicate task. So if Mike would not voluntarily provide a statement then he might need to be subpoenaed.

A few evenings later, Frank received a call from Vic Gibbs.

"Are you in the Minster this evening?"

Frank had been undecided as his usual drinking buddy Dick was away for the day at a regimental reunion, but Vic was always good company.

"I can be, if you are."

"Great. I'll see you there at about six."

Frank arrived to find Vic already awaiting him with a pint. They exchanged pleasantries and Vic then launched straight in.

"I was in your office on Tuesday to meet Dick on a job we've got on together and I noticed Ronnie Best and his mate Glen coming out of your room."

Frank nodded but said nothing, not wanting to breach confidentiality.

"You know they're a couple of crooks – one big crook and one little one."

Frank didn't quite know how to react to this. He could see why a financial adviser like Vic who stuck to the rules would resent the likes of Ronnie and Glen. He would do his best to arrange a mortgage for borderline cases. If he was unsuccessful, he would usually earn nothing. The client might then find his or her way to Ronnie or Glen who would arrange the finance for someone who was not eligible and, more often than not, could not afford to repay it. In doing so, they would earn more on one case than Vic would earn on five legitimate ones.

"Do you know Ronnie Best operates a huge web of dodgy introducers? He is the black widow at the centre of the web," he uttered with relish, warming to the metaphor. "And caught in the web are dodgy surveyors who overvalue the properties, suppliers of dodgy references and false payslips, dodgy estate agents who represent residential buy-to-lets as family homes, and the less said about Mike Roberts the better.

"I just don't want you to get drawn into his web. You don't need his sort of contacts. You don't want to ruin your reputation before you've got one."

"Don't worry, Vic," replied Frank. "I obviously can't breach client confidentiality, but he isn't asking me to deal with any conveyancing and I wouldn't if he did. I don't do conveyancing anyway."

As he said this, Vic's gaze drifted to the entrance and his face lit up.

"Guildford-Brown, my man," he exclaimed with the tone of mock theatricality he always adopted when Dick was around.

"Glad I've caught up with you. I didn't know if you'd still be about. Well, I've really disgraced myself now."

Dick's pint of best rapidly materialised on the bar to the evident irritation of a less-favoured group still waiting to be served. He sank half of it without uttering another word while Frank and Vic waited expectantly.

"You remember, Frank, how drenched we were after lunch yesterday?"

Frank remembered it well. They had lunched at a more distant hostelry and were returning to the office through torrential rain with some haste. Dick had an early afternoon appointment with one of the firm's most prestigious clients, Lady Pendoggett. She was a personal client of Charles McCullough, the firm's founder and senior partner. Lady Pendoggett was the joint owner with her elderly husband, Sir Evelyn Pendoggett, of the Pendoggett estate, comprising two stately homes in varying states of disrepair, several dozen cottages and six-hundred acres of rolling Cornish farmland. She required independent advice before signing a deed mortgaging the estate to Coutts bank to raise funds for Sir Evelyn's new business venture – the development of part of the estate as a golf course, club house and farm shops.

Charles McCullough had spent many years wooing Sir Evelyn as a client. This required the wresting away of the estate from its long-standing legal advisers – Cornwall's largest firm which had represented it for several generations. He had finally succeeded just before the commencement of the most substantial piece of legal business the estate had embarked upon for decades – and he let everyone know it.

Charles was not a man known for his sense of humour and it had been made plain to Dick that this was his most important client and that none of his usual knock-about tom-foolery was required.

"Don't try to get her drunk, don't perform the Agincourt scene and, most importantly, no monkey impersonations," was the firm instruction.

Not for the first time, Dick had accepted one last pint and was cutting it very fine. Dick was as fit as a fiddle and trusted to his long, loose-limbed frame to get him back in time. He and Frank had ended up jogging back through the deluge across perilously slippery pavements, and in endeavouring to take a corner at speed, Dick had skidded spectacularly, ending up supine and spread-eagled in a large puddle.

Safely back in the office, Dick was faced with the problem of making respectable the soaking trousers of his pinstripe suit in the five minutes available before the arrival of his most important client ever. Frank recalled the mounting sense of panic.

"I remember it well. I assume you did your usual and dried your trousers over your trusty radiator."

Dick's office was blessed with a substantial partner's desk to which he had entrusted the preservation of his modesty on several similar occasions in the past. Debs would bring the client through and they would never know that their respected solicitor had conducted the entirety of their interview in his underpants.

"That I did," said Dick. "And they were steaming away nicely. I had relaxed into my chair and taken a call from a client which distracted me slightly and Debs had buzzed through to announce the arrival of her Ladyship. 'Bring her through, Debs,' I said without thinking."

"The difficulty with officer training in Her Majesty's Services is that it tries to make a gentleman of you, and as

Debs opened the door and ushered her Ladyship through, I was on my feet around my desk and advancing across the room with my arm extended to greet her."

Vic had seen the way this was going and let out a great guttural guffaw. Frank looked on in horrified disbelief.

"It was then that I looked over her shoulder and noticed my trousers still steaming nicely on the radiator and the horrible realisation dawned. I dipped back around my desk but it was too late, the damage was done. How could I explain to Charles the loss of our most important client?

"But, Lady Pendoggett is not the humourless harridan our esteemed senior partner believes her to be...

"'Fine pair of legs there, Mr Guildford-Brown,' she said. 'Do you get them out for all your clients or just those with titles?'

"Well, what could I say?

"'I'm most awfully sorry, Lady Pendoggett,' I bumbled. 'I had completely forgotten that my trousers were drying over the radiator.' I waved in their general direction.

"'You had forgotten you had no trousers on? Are you normally so absent-minded in matters of dress and decorum? I hope you are not so absent-minded when conducting your legal work.'

"Her manner was schoolmarm-ly and scolding, and yet her eyes belied this. It was obvious she was trying very hard not to smile.

"'Certainly not in legal matters, Lady Pendoggett, as I hope will become evident, and I do hope you won't find the need to mention this to Mr McCullough?'

"'Why should I? I don't think he would find this anywhere near as amusing as I do,' she said, now beaming openly. 'And not so much of the Lady Pendoggett. My friends call me Lucinda or Lady P. I think I'm going to like you, Mr Guildford-Brown.'"

By this time, Frank felt distinctly relieved and Vic was convulsed and slumped against the bar.

"Well, I'm glad I've amused you," said Dick, slightly indignantly. "Your round then."

Three weeks later, Frank arrived in the Plymouth County Court at 9 am for a pre-hearing conference with counsel. At 10.30 am the court was reviewing its original decision to freeze the sale and hear Glen's application to discharge it on the basis that his wife's claim should apply to the sale proceeds, still held in Mike Roberts' client account, and not to the hotel itself.

Glen was waiting in the foyer. Bob, the witness to the deed, and the conveyancer, Mike Roberts, had been subpoenaed as witnesses. Frank had taken statements from both and trusted neither. Bob claimed that he had witnessed Mrs Terrell's signature, the signature she claimed had never happened. Frank did not believe him when he took his statement, and he could not believe Bob would be any more convincing on oath before the judge, being cross-examined by Mrs Terrell's counsel.

Mike Roberts was a little harder to fathom. What instructions had he received from Mrs Terrell?

No one disputed that she had originally asked him to proceed with the sale. And as she ran the business she had provided most of the information required to reply to the buyers' solicitors' enquiries. In his statement, taken by Frank on a visit to the office of Roberts & Co a few weeks previously, Mike had denied receiving any instructions from Margot, countermanding her original agreement to the sale. If he had received such instructions, he would not of course have completed it, he had told Frank.

According to Margot's witness statement, she had left a phone message with the Roberts & Co receptionist to put the sale on hold until further notice. This, Mike claimed, had never reached him.

When Frank had discussed this with Dick, who, as a conveyancer, dealt with Mike's office regularly, Dick had said that this was entirely believable. Mike's office, it seemed, was run on a shoestring, with insufficient, untrained and disinterested staff.

At his meeting with Mike, Frank had asked if he could have a look through Mike's conveyancing file. At least he could check if it contained an attendance note of Margot's conversation with the receptionist. He had been told that this was not possible, as the police had turned up unannounced at his office with a warrant for its production a few days earlier and made off with it.

The only other witness was Derek Harvey. Glen had been appalled at the prospect of his solicitor issuing a witness summons against the head of Plymouth's leading crime family. Frank had advised them that they needed Derek as a witness to show that he was an innocent buyer and had not colluded with Glen to provide a "stool pigeon" willing to give false evidence of Margot's signature.

Fortunately, there had been no need. Derek had resisted pressure from his sons to allow them to sort out the problem without recourse to the law and had applied to be joined as a party in the case to demonstrate his own innocence. He was attending the hearing with his own solicitor and barrister. The downside of this was that he had let Glen know that he was expected to pay their fees – whether the court ordered it or not.

Frank was pleased to have engaged his first choice of barrister – Jemima Goldman. He had thought initially that he might have problems justifying his choice to his chauvinistic client and his moderately less sexist friend. Jemima was in her early thirties, but looked younger, and her exotic demeanour set her apart in the local courts. But her mind was razor-sharp, her cross-examination polite but deadly and no one doubted that she would be a QC before the age of forty.

Glen and Ronnie, who was paying, accepted his recommendation. Frank introduced her to Glen in the interview room. As usual, she wasted no time on pleasantries.

"So, Mr Terrell, unless your wife can prove that the buyer was complicit with you in the production of forged documents, my view is that there is a good chance the judge will discharge the injunction in so far as it relates to the hotel, but order that it remains in place in relation to the sale proceeds and leave your wife to make her claim on that. But as in all cases, there is an element of uncertainty. The court will not hear evidence from the witnesses today nor will the witnesses be cross-examined. The judge will simply read their statements. And if the judge then thinks that the buyer has assisted in some way with the production of forged documents, such as by providing malleable witnesses prepared to give false evidence, or if, even without believing that, the judge thinks that your wife genuinely wishes to keep the hotel and should be given the opportunity to argue for its retention at the final hearing, then it is always possible the judge will maintain the current injunction in place until then."

"But she admits she accepted the sale price and asked Mr Roberts to go ahead with the sale?"

"She does, but she is always entitled to change her mind up to the time contracts are exchanged."

"Well, if the court does that I'm a dead man. Can't you tell the judge that?"

"I can, but we would need some evidence. And even though the court can consider the effect of its order on an innocent third party, it wouldn't normally take into account the fact that a third party it doesn't consider to be innocent, doesn't much like its order. Anyway, that party is now joined in the proceedings, so can make that point to the court itself."

"So what can I do to get out of this mess?"

"Offer her something more from the sale proceeds to drop the case."

"But then she will have won; stitched me up and got more than she deserves."

"Well, it's your choice, Mr Terrell – your principles or your peace of mind. Every lawyer will tell you it's not worth going to court over a principle; and if you do believe the Harveys are a threat to your safety then you should contact the police."

Glen looked distraught.

Jemima now turned to Frank.

"How far apart are we, Frank?"

"Well, the net sale proceeds are £318,000. There is a Capital Gains Tax liability of £19,000, leaving approximately £299,000, of which Glen has already offered her 60%."

"Which she agreed," interjected Glen.

"She now wants 75%, so we are arguing over £45,000."

"Right," exclaimed Jemima. "So tell me, Mr Terrell, how much of that are you willing to pay to be sure of getting the Harveys off your back?"

"I'd pay them all of it. They paid £100,000 more than it was worth anyway. I just don't want to pay it to her."

Frank felt he should intervene.

"We don't want to pressurise you into settling if you really don't want to, Glen."

"I do want to settle, I do," spluttered Glen.

"Well, the only way to do that is to offer her more of the sale proceeds now. Look at it this way, you've still got the divorce proceedings to go through."

"Exactly, and she'll be after more money from me then."

"That's the point I'm trying to make – the bigger the share of the family assets she has now, the less will be available for her to claim against then."

"So are you saying we can get it back from her then?"

"It won't be as clear-cut as that, but if the matrimonial finances end up before the court, the judge will look at the value of the assets each party already has in deciding how to divide up what's left."

Glen thought for a moment. A devious smile flickered across his face.

"So if we give her more now, she might not have won after all and I might get the Harveys off my back. So how much should we offer her?"

Frank glanced across at Jemima, who had been looking on silently as Frank endeavoured to soften their client's pigheadedness.

"Well, why don't Frank and I meet with your wife's

advisers and see if we can reach a settlement? Of course, we won't commit to anything without your agreement."

"OK, good luck with that; but she won't concede a penny."

Jemima rapped imperiously on the door of Interview Room 4. A few seconds later, the elegant head of Margot's counsel peered out.

"Can we have a word please?"

"Of course, my dear, of course. Just a moment."

Piers Fulton could only be a barrister. Frank had noticed him around court – you couldn't fail to. Immaculate in navy blue pinstripe with a fob watch, his slightly puffy jowls and ruddy complexion had the look of a man who enjoyed the good things in life. Looked at alongside his own counsel, an uninformed observer might well think that Mrs Terrell had got the better of her husband in the choice of advocate. But Piers had embarked upon his legal career with the best contacts in the world. His father had been a High Court judge, and most of the present judiciary on the Western Circuit had known him as a young man. Yet here he was, in his early forties, pottering around the Plymouth County Court taking on any case that came his way.

Piers was followed out of the room by his instructing solicitor, a specialist family practitioner and a young man in his early twenties who appeared the perfect clone of Piers.

"I am sure you both know my instructing solicitor, Geraldine," he announced with a hint of pomposity. "But you may not have met my pupil, Giles Pomroy. Giles, this is Jemima Goldman, one of our most formidable young lady advocates." Jemima nodded dismissively, ignoring the proffered hand.

"So, Jemima, what have you got to offer me?"

Thirty minutes later, Jemima and Frank were back in Interview Room 1.

"She will accept an extra £10,000 and agree that the injunction be discharged with each party paying their own costs," Jemima announced with her characteristic languid delivery.

"Crikey! I'm amazed. How did you manage that?"

"First of all they asked for £30,000. We offered nothing on the basis that the court was bound to discharge the injunction as it prejudiced an innocent buyer. They backtracked surprisingly quickly. Perhaps Piers didn't have the stomach for it," she added as an aside to Frank.

Frank pondered for a moment, then asked Glen.

"Do you think it's possible that the Harveys could have got at Margot?"

"Anything's possible, but I don't think Derek would threaten a woman. With the boys, who knows? Does it mean that if I agree to this, the sale can go ahead straight away?"

"Yes, immediately."

"Right, great, go ahead then. I agree."

A fortnight later, Frank and Dick were at their usual place at the bar of the Minster.

"You'll never guess who I saw lunching at The Cornucopia," Dick whispered secretively.

"Go on then, tell me; but first tell me who you were lunching with at such great expense."

"Well, if you must know, it was that doyenne of the Cornish county set, Lady Pendoggett."

"Ha, ha, she of the steaming-trousers disaster. I would

have thought she was much too staid for a Guildford-Brown lunch partner."

"Well, she's not as staid as all that. But I had no choice – lunch at The Cornucopia was her price for not relaying the news of yours truly's humiliation to our esteemed senior partner, but you'll be intrigued to know who else was there."

"Go on then, who?"

"Our dodgy fellow solicitor Mike Roberts, in an amorous liaison with the wife of your client Glen Terrell."

"You mean Margot?"

"That's the one."

"How amorous?"

"Very. Holding hands, gazing entranced into each other's eyes over the lobster salad. You should have seen the poor sod's expression when he saw me there. Quite ruined his day, it did. I bet he thought twenty-five miles up the Tamar Valley on a Tuesday lunchtime he'd be safe from prying eyes.

"I couldn't resist going over and passing the time of day. He introduced her as a business colleague but I knew better."

"Well, what a tangled web. I wonder if Glen knows."

Glen did know. The following day he was on the phone to the office requesting an urgent appointment that afternoon.

He turned up with his faithful confidant Ronnie and wearing a dejected hang-dog look.

"Well, I've really been stitched up by one of your lot," he began.

Not wishing to give the impression that Margot's infidelity was the talk of the town, Frank feigned innocence.

"I'm being – what is it, Ronnie?"

"Cuckolded," said Ronnie, with a dramatic relish worthy of Vic Gibbs. "You're being cuckolded. Cuckolded by an Officer of the Supreme Court."

"OK, don't take the piss, Ronnie."

"Sorry, Glen."

"Which of my colleagues in the legal profession are we talking about?" Frank asked.

"That bastard Mike Roberts; my solicitor knocking off my wife."

"I'm sorry to hear that, Glen."

"I know he's a good-looking bastard and a flash git, but there must be rules against going off with your client's wife. Who can I report him to?"

"Um, the Law Society, possibly."

"Tell him the rest of it, Glen," prompted Ronnie.

"Yes, well, it's worse than that. Ronnie's got some friends in the force; regulars at the Captain Flint and Ronnie's new girly bar."

"Ronnie's Review Bar," announced Ronnie proudly. "Late-night club licence and best girls in the city. You're welcome as a guest any time, Frank."

"I might take that up," said Frank, not wishing to offend.

"You know the fuzz turned up unannounced at Roberts & Co and took the file?" said Glen.

"Before Mike could doctor it," chimed in Ronnie, still appearing to relish the whole affair.

"My criminal solicitor had asked for a copy of the whole file so that we would know what we were up against. But the police were sitting on it and we thought we would need to apply for a court order for disclosure. So I told Ronnie and he said he would make a few enquiries."

Ronnie could not resist taking over.

"I asked my mates in the force and they gave me some interesting information. First, there is a note on the file detailing Margot's call to the office telling Mike's receptionist, Tina, that she'd thought some more about Mike's suggestion of the previous day and agreed with it. It didn't say what that suggestion was. Also, on the file is a Land Registry transfer deed signed by Margot and witnessed by Mike Roberts."

"Which hadn't been passed to the buyers on completion?" asked Frank.

"No, they were given the other one, witnessed by Bob, which Margot denies signing.

"But the plot thickens," said Ronnie happily. "Mike's receptionist Tina has taken a bit of a shine to him, and she had got wind of the goings on with Margot which she didn't like one bit – and she has given a statement to the police. She knew exactly what Mike's suggestion was.

"The day after Margot had called into the office, Tina had picked Mike up from a lunch with that developer guy Danny. Mike acts for all his buyers and they're great mates. Anyway, they were both pissed as handcarts and Tina was taking Mike back to the office to sign his post and then dropping him back to the pub. Mike was telling Danny about this wizard wheeze he'd thought up.

"These clients of his had split up and were selling their business to the Harveys and everyone knows you can't let down the Harveys. They had agreed to a division of the sale proceeds, but the wife wanted more – and she would reward Mike handsomely, in any way he wanted, if he could arrange it. So they let the completion of the sale happen and relieved the Harveys of their money and then, straight after completion and before the Harveys had got their purchase registered at the Land Registry, the wife expressed horrified disbelief that the sale had gone through, denied having executed the transfer deed, alleged forgery and applied to the court to freeze the sale. So if the wife had not signed it then the implication was that the husband must have forged it and the Harveys would know who to come after. Only another fifty grand would get them off his back, ten grand for Mike and the rest for the wife.

"They thought they were whispering in the back of Tina's car, but like all drunks, they talked too loudly and Tina could hear every word. That was their undoing because Tina's cousin is married to Denny Harvey and it wasn't long before the Harveys knew who the real villain was – and it wasn't Glen. So the boys called in at Mike's office and had a quiet word with him, and at the last hearing, Margot dropped the whole thing."

"We did wonder, didn't we?" said Frank. "Whether the Harveys had got at Margot, but it was Mike they got at."

Frank thought for a moment.

"So this is good news, Glen, and there seems little point in reporting Mike Roberts to the Law Society as I imagine that once the police find out they will arrest both Mike and Margot for conspiracy to pervert the course of justice."

"Yes," said Glen. "That's what Harry Paget says, and the police do know because Tina has given them a statement. They've told Harry informally that the forgery charges against me will be dropped."

"So more good news then."

"Yeah, but I want my ten grand back."

"That may not be easy."

"Why, have you given it to her yet?"

"No, but I have given an undertaking to her matrimonial solicitors to send it to them as soon as the Harveys' title to the hotel is registered at the Land Registry, and as Ronnie will tell you, a solicitor's undertaking is sacred."

Glen smiled smugly.

"But I think if you ask them they might let you off it; if I confirm I won't give evidence against Margot."

"We need to be careful," said Frank, after a moment's thought. "Not to seem to be blackmailing them. But I suppose if we say that we don't want to further aggravate the matrimonial issues between you by giving evidence against her, then the police might just be willing to treat it as a civil matter. I don't think they'll let Mike off the hook though, given his status as a solicitor. I think their view will be that their public duty obliges them to prosecute."

"I don't give a damn about Mike Roberts. He can go to the dogs. Let's see if Margot wants to continue a relationship with a struck-off solicitor."

So it turned out, after a call by Frank, Margot's solicitors confirmed she would forego the extra £10,000 and Frank was released from his undertaking. The Crown Prosecution Service agreed to drop all charges against Glen. No proceedings were brought against Margot, but Mike was arrested and charged with conspiracy.

Frank never did take up Ronnie's invitation to The Review Bar, but six weeks or so later, Frank, Dick and Nell bumped into Ronnie at the official opening of a new estate agency. The group was too small to allow Frank to avoid him, as he would have preferred. Ronnie, as always, seemed delighted to see them.

"I bet you don't see cases like that every day? What a tangled web!"

Coming from Ronnie, who was not averse to spinning the odd tangled web himself, this was rich.

"No, thank God, I don't. So what's Glen up to now?"

"Still arranging mortgages, some for me and some on his own account, and setting up his new financial advisers' business. He'll probably be on to you for some client recommendations soon."

Not in a thousand years, thought Frank.

"I suppose if I tell you something about him you're still bound by client confidentiality and all that? You wouldn't pass it on?"

Frank could see what was coming.

"Yes, that's correct. Unless you tell me that he's about to take out a contract on the life of his wife, that is."

"Ha, ha, he probably would if he knew someone who'd take it on. No, it's not that; it's about the transfer deed – you know, he forged it. He signed Margot's name, he knew her signature as he'd been doing it for years, and bunged Bob two-hundred quid to witness it."

"Well, no, of course I didn't know that, but frankly I'm not all that surprised. I think that's exactly what Mike and Margot thought he would do. No solicitor in his right mind would give a deed to one party in a marriage break-up to arrange for the other to sign. They set him up for it and he fell right into their hands."

"As I said," beamed Ronnie, "what a tangled web."

Part Five

Neighbours from Hell and Dangerous Dogs

Dick's brush with the firm's most important client turned out not to be the disaster he had feared after all. In fact, Lady Pendoggett reported to Charles McCullough, the firm's senior partner, that she had been more than satisfied with Mr Guildford-Brown's services. Charles had telephoned Dick to announce that the firm had now received instructions to act for the Pendoggett estate in its mega development scheme.

For a few months thereafter, business was fairly uneventful with the clientele being drawn from the humdrum mass of decent humankind. And, then, without warning, two bizarre cases descended on poor Frank at the same time.

The first of these emerged from that dustbin of many promising legal careers, the neighbourhood dispute. Old lawyers with a little seniority and influence within their firms will generally decline such cases. But Frank still had a career to make. He had to take on whatever came in. He had also never done one before, though he knew enough about them to realise they were best avoided. So when he came into work that morning and saw written in his diary, "10 am Mr & Mrs Lemon, neighbourhood dispute", he resolved to grit his teeth and give it his best shot.

Mr and Mrs Lemon were a well-turned-out middle-aged couple who kept a grocery shop in one of Plymouth's better-off suburbs. They looked as if they could have been brother and sister. Both were a little short and dumpy, neatly if conservatively dressed; they had worn their best clothes to come and see him. He could sense their nervous tension – this interview was important to them. His first task was to put them at ease.

"Thank you for coming in to see me, Mr and Mrs Lemon. I am Mr Gilbert, or Frank if you would prefer." He had the feeling they would not prefer and were more comfortable with formality. "I understand you have a problem with a neighbour. Would you like to tell me about it?"

His clients glanced at one another. Mrs Lemon nodded to her husband who began.

"Yes, and thank you for seeing us, Mr Gilbert. We have the misfortune to live next door to what I believe is commonly referred to as the neighbour from hell."

"I am very sorry to hear that," said Frank.

Mr Lemon's clipped vowels, reminiscent of a Dickensian shopkeeper, did nothing to dilute the initial impression that this male client, at least, was a little ridiculous.

Mr Lemon pressed on.

"We live in a very nice detached house in Plymchurch which we bought six years ago as it was near the busier of our two grocery shops. Our other shop is in Olverston," he added with a hint of pride.

"Just around the corner from where Lawrence of Arabia used to live," added his wife, who did not seem to share her husband's sense of gravity. "When we moved in, we had lovely neighbours on both sides," she continued. "Two retired couples – very quiet, no trouble at all. We used to help each other out all the time. Our neighbours on the right moved out when the husband died and the house was too big for an elderly lady on her own. A couple in their thirties, Mr and Mrs Clarke, moved in with their two teenage daughters – a bit noisy but basically OK. We have had to politely ask them to keep the noise down a few times, and they always try to and apologise for inconveniencing us."

Mr Lemon then took over, seeming to feel that the serious bits were his responsibility.

"But then last year the Haddocks moved in on the other side and that was the end of our peaceful existence." He paused balefully.

"The first thing to go wrong was that Mr Haddock began parking his huge builder's van on our shared drive – he has a building firm, Haddock Construction. We each own half of the drive but his van was too wide to fit in his half and jutted over into ours, so there was no room for our little Renault. I asked him politely if he wouldn't mind parking it on the road as it was too big for the drive and after a lot of grumbling he moved it. But then I would come home a few days later and it would be there again. What was especially annoying was that his wife's BMW, which itself was a big car but not too wide to fit on his half of the drive, was always parked on the road."

Frank could see this was going to be a long job.

"Could I organise you a cup of tea?"

"No, no, thanks very much, but I need to get this off my chest."

Despite his wife's obvious disappointment, he pressed on.

"I could tell each time I asked him to move he was becoming more and more irritated, and finally, on about the fourth or fifth occasion, he snapped a point-blank refusal.

"He told me it wasn't his fault if I couldn't get my little car up the drive. He said he was fed up with being hassled by me every time he got home from a hard day's work, and he told me in no uncertain terms to go away. In fact, his language was much coarser than that and his wife came out and told him to stop swearing and go indoors.

"The next few days when I arrived home, also after a hard day's work, I hasten to add – just because I work in a shop and not a building site, doesn't mean I don't work hard." He glanced up at Frank as if seeking support and Frank nodded encouragingly.

"He was parked on the drive," he continued. "Even though there was space on the road.

"I decided to avoid another argument and parked on the road myself.

"But it rankled. I lay awake at night thinking, why shouldn't I park on my drive? I owned half of it. I wasn't going to be bullied. The next evening there he was, on the drive again – on part of my half. So I reversed my car carefully along the drive with the driver's side wheels on the garden verge. I knew I might destroy some of my plants but it would be worth it."

As he said this, he looked sheepishly across at his wife as if confessing to some as yet undiscovered crime.

"The passenger side of my vehicle was now tight up against his driver's door. His passenger side was tight against the shed. The van was therefore inaccessible. I slipped out of my car and tiptoed through my flower bed with a sense of enormous satisfaction and waited for the storm.

"It was not long in coming. Thirty minutes or so later, there was a banging on the front door. I opened it to a torrent of abuse.

"'What do you effing well mean by blocking my van door? Come out and move your effing car right now!'

"'I'm very sorry, Mr Haddock, but it's you who has caused the problem by parking your van on my part of the drive. You're surely not suggesting that I'm not entitled to park on my half?'

"The quiet reasonableness with which I said this only seemed to irritate him more. His face distorted with rage.

"'You're asking for a slap, you little git!' he fairly screamed at me. 'Move your effing car now. I've got an urgent call out.'

"'You've now threatened me on my own doorstep and Mr and Mrs Clarke have witnessed it.'

"I pointed over his shoulder at our neighbours, who had been watering their garden and were now peering over the hedge in alarm.

"'You leave me no choice but to call the police,' I told him solemnly.

"I tried to close the front door but he had blocked it with his large builder's boot. So with the door still open and Mr Haddock still raging at the door, I picked up the phone and dialled the Plymchurch Police Station and reported a breach of the peace.

"While I was doing this, I heard Mrs Haddock calling her husband and he disappeared back down the pathway, calling me an effing git as he went.

"To my surprise, the police turned up, and very quickly too. A very nice young man, PC Willman, who didn't look old enough to be out of school. He spoke to us, then to Mr Haddock, who I could see was arguing with him. Then he spoke to Mr and Mrs Clark who I could see didn't really want to get involved. I think they are a bit afraid of Mr Haddock; he isn't that tall but he's very burly and has an aggressive, overbearing manner. The constable then spoke to Mr Haddock again, who looked furious. Afterwards he came back to tell me that he could plainly see that Mr Haddock's vehicle was partially obstructing our side of the drive and he had told him to move it. But he went on to say that if this happened again there wouldn't be much he could do about it as trespass was a civil matter and we would need to consult a solicitor. But he had also told Mr Haddock that threatening his neighbour with physical violence could constitute common assault, and if further threats were made which lead to a breach of the peace, then he risked arrest. He told me he would log this incident in police records so that his colleagues would be aware of it if called again and my solicitor could obtain a police report if matters went further.

"Things went quiet for a week or so. His van stayed on the road and there were no more arguments – we simply ignored each other. Until, that is, the hot tubs turned up.

"We got back from the shop one Friday evening and there were two enormous hot tubs in the Haddock's back garden, with Mr and Mrs Haddock in one of them as it bubbled away. We had no objection to this in itself, although when Mr Haddock emerged from the tub sporting the most miniscule trunks imaginable – Speedos, I believe they're called; budgie-smugglers, I call them – I felt I should put my hand over my daughter's eyes.

"But, the following evening, cars began to appear in the road, and hordes of party-going visitors, most of them struggling with huge bags of clinking bottles, piled into next door. The music started up – a horrible thumping racket which must have been audible for miles around. They all piled into the front door fully clothed, and in no time at all they were out of the back door and into the garden in their swimwear – if you could call it that, some of the women were wearing almost nothing at all. And as the evening went on and the drink flowed, some of them lost their tops and were chased, screaming and giggling, around the garden and in and out of the house by the men. It looked like a right orgy.

"I put up with it until about midnight, but by then I'd had enough. I wasn't willing to embarrass myself by going round to complain and getting a lot of abuse. So I phoned the police but they didn't answer. I wanted to call the police again, but Sheila, that's Mrs Lemon, insisted I didn't. She said our relationship with them was bad enough already and it might just be a housewarming and there might not be any more. But there were – every few weeks or so. Not as big as the first one but the same three or four couples running around the back garden, in and out of the hot tubs, screaming and shouting and playing loud music until three or four in the morning."

"You could complain to the local authority," Frank suggested. "They have powers to deal with noisy neighbours under the Control of Pollution Act."

"I have done and they gave me a noise recording machine but it doesn't come over so loud on tape and they seem reluctant to do anything."

"Which is why you're here?"

"It is, but there's more. A few months ago we went away on a fortnight's holiday – mainly to get away from Mr Haddock. We had a great time, didn't we, Sheila?"

Sheila nodded. "We did, dear."

"But leaving your house empty with a lunatic living next door leaves you rather apprehensive on the return journey as to what you'll find when you get back. And sure enough, our neighbour from hell hadn't been idle. I stepped into my back garden and to my horror a two-storey wooden structure loomed up against our boundary. While we had been on holiday, our nightmare neighbours had constructed a huge building in their back garden, blocking out our light and our view over Plymview Woods. Builders can obviously move fast if they want to," he concluded wryly.

"That sounds like it might have needed planning permission," Frank suggested.

"Yes, absolutely, it did. Someone came round from the planning department. She confirmed immediately that it needed permission. It was a permanent structure, two storeys high and right up against our boundary. She was also very interested when I told her our neighbours are Haddock Construction, who are apparently well-known to the planning department. She said they would write to him telling him he needed retrospective permission or would have to demolish it. We would have notice of the application and the right to object, so we did."

"On what grounds?"

"It was too big – overdevelopment, I think they call it – and it adversely affected our amenities – it blocked out our light and view. We tried to get other neighbours to object. I think one or two did but most didn't want to get involved – as

I said, they're scared of him. But it didn't matter because his planning application was refused.

"We were delighted when the council told us and we looked forward to seeing the monstrosity come down.

"But, the following evening, there was a hammering on our front door. We knew it was him and Sheila told me to ignore it, but I wasn't going to be a prisoner in my own home. I answered the door and there he was, larger than life.

"'You interfering nosy bastard – think you've won, don't you?' He spoke quietly to avoid attracting attention from the Clarkes, but his rage was obvious and barely suppressed.

"'It isn't a matter of winning,' I replied calmly. 'It's a matter of sticking up for normal civilised behaviour. The planning laws are there to protect decent people from bullies – and that's why your monstrosity is coming down.'

"'Like hell it is. I'm taking on specialist planning lawyers – I can afford them, unlike you – and my appeal's going in next week.'

"With this, he raised a finger at me and stormed off down the path, calling over his shoulder as he went, 'And we've got some good parties planned.'"

"Which is, as I said, why you're here."

"Which is why we're here, Mr Gilbert. If he does appeal and wins, what other rights do we have?"

Frank thought for a moment.

"Well, first of all, this threat to appeal may just be a bluff. Planning appeals are expensive, specialist planning lawyers are expensive and, contrary to public opinion, most lawyers will tell him not to bother if they think it has little chance of success. As for your other rights, were both your houses built at roughly the same time?"

"Yes, I'm sure they were. Is that relevant?"

"It could be. I would need to see a copy of your Land Registry title – do you have a copy at home?"

"I do, and annoyingly I nearly brought it with me."

"Well, if you could drop it in some time. I want to see if it says anything about rights of light and what covenants might exist. It would be very useful if your neighbours' title is subject to a covenant not to cause nuisance or annoyance to the neighbours."

From looking utterly crestfallen, Mr Lemon was now perking up considerably.

"Excellent, I'm sure I've seen something like that in our deeds. So, they might be in his too?"

"They might. If the same developer built the houses and sold them off at the same time then his solicitor may well have imposed identical covenants."

"And rights of light, you say?"

"Possibly, does the new building block light to any of your windows, or just the garden?"

"It blocks the light to our kitchen window for much of the day, and also our view."

"The view might be more difficult. There is no general right to a view, but blocking one might be a breach of covenant not to cause a nuisance."

By this time Mr Lemon was having difficulty containing his excitement.

"Brilliant, so I'll drop in our deeds tomorrow and then what happens?"

"Subject to what they say, I can write to Mr and Mrs

Haddock, pointing out that their conduct constitutes a breach of those covenants and an infringement of your right to light."

"Excellent, and what if he ignores it? Which he will."

"The next stage might be a threat of court proceedings for an order preventing the nuisance – called an injunction – and to take down the offending building. But that's a little way off yet."

But it wasn't far off for Mr Lemon, who was on his feet and shaking hands in his impatience to consult his deeds.

"Thank you ever so much, Mr Gilbert. You've restored my confidence in the English legal system, hasn't he, dear?"

Frank did not hear whether Mrs Lemon agreed as her husband had already bundled her out of the door.

No sooner had they left when Debs buzzed through to say that his friend Alec, of the Plymouth Sound crossing fame, had phoned several times sounding rather agitated, and could Frank phone him back immediately. He dictated a long note of his interview with the Lemons and then did so.

The Lemons' problem, despite being thorny and incapable of easy resolution, was a common one. Alec's was not.

Alec lived in a smallholding on the foothills of Bodmin Moor with his wife, Drusilla. Drusilla and Alec had recently married and Frank did not know her well. He was aware though, from his only visit, that she kept several large and particularly ferocious-looking dogs, Rhodesian Ridgebacks, lion-hunting dogs, as Alec had told Frank. The farm was remote, Alec was often away from work and the dogs were an excellent disincentive to intruders.

But they plainly had not deterred the village postman.

One of the bitches, Potentilla by name, had had puppies. This particular postman, rather than avoiding dogs of any size, as most sensible postmen do, fancied himself as a bit of a dog whisperer. The dogs and their kennel were enclosed in a pen high enough to prevent the puppies from wandering, but not too high to prevent access by a fit young postman.

Drusilla had watched the postman from her upstairs window as he leant across the fence to fraternise with the puppies – even Ridgebacks were cute at that age. She watched with slightly more concern as he reached down over the fence to smooth them. He would surely notice their mother's taut, tense demeanour and back off; she could move like lightning if she felt the need and unlike most dogs, real hunters did not bark a warning. It seemed that he had, as he withdrew his arm and stepped backwards.

Rather than calling him from the window to warn him that Ridgeback mothers should be treated with respect, she decided to go down. She had just reached the bottom of the stairs when she heard the scream. Within seconds she was outside and across the yard. The postman was rolling on the floor, clutching his groin, still screaming.

"She bit me, the bloody bitch bit me!"

Drusilla had a reputation for not suffering fools gladly.

"Well, what the hell were you doing? You could see she had new puppies?"

"I just stepped over the fence to smooth them, pick one up perhaps. I had one leg over the fence and she was on me," he sobbed. "God knows what she's done to me, I could be maimed."

"You bloody idiot. Why do you think we put the fence up?"

With this, she noticed an expanding bloodstain on his trousers and thought perhaps she should show a bit more sympathy.

"OK, let me drive you to Plymouth Hospital. Can you walk?"

"No, call an ambulance – I could be maimed forever. I haven't had children yet. What will I say to my wife?"

Reluctantly Drusilla did as he asked, and forty minutes later the still-traumatised postman was whisked away by concerned-looking paramedics. She suspected this was not the last she would hear of it.

She was right. Alec had known nothing about the incident until he returned home from work that evening to find a police car pulling out of the drive. Drusilla told him all the grizzly details.

Two officers had turned up with a dog-handling unit to assess whether Potentilla constituted a continuing risk and should be removed. Drusilla had been interviewed under caution and expressed the view, perhaps unwisely, that the postman was the author of his own misfortune. If he had simply done his job by placing their letters in the post box, and not wandered around private property looking for trouble, he would have left in the same perfect condition he had arrived in. Instead, he had tried to climb over the barrier into the enclosed dog pen to pet newborn puppies in the presence of their large and formidable mother.

Drusilla had told the police that, in her view, this came as close to an act of intentional self-harm as she could imagine. The police had not known about the puppies. Fortunately, in Drusilla's view, the dog handlers, unlike the postman, had understood dogs. In their presence, she had entered the enclosure, picked up a couple of puppies and handed them over the fence to the dog handlers to pet and talk soothingly to. Potentilla had eyed them intently but made no move.

Eventually, satisfied that she probably only constituted a threat to anyone climbing uninvited into the enclosure, the police agreed not to remove her on condition that Drusilla arranged to erect a sign on the front gate, which they provided, warning of the dog's presence. Before they left though, they did warn her that she might well be prosecuted for keeping a dangerous dog and that the court would have power to order the dog's removal or destruction.

Alec related all this to Frank on the phone.

"Have you heard how the postman is?" Frank enquired.

"No news yet."

"Well, you ought to check if you're covered for this on your house insurance – or any specialist pet or livestock insurance."

Alec thought they were, at least they had been when their bullocks had destroyed a neighbour's fence a few years back. Other than notifying their insurers, they agreed to sit tight for the moment and await the oncoming storm.

A few days later, the Land Registry title to the Lemons' house arrived on Frank's desk. As expected, the title contained a fairly standard covenant not to cause excessive noise and not to cause nuisance or annoyance to neighbours. Also included was a restriction against parking on the shared driveway so as to block their neighbours' access. There was no surrender of the property's rights of light over the adjoining properties, so if, as the Lemons stated, the new building did block the light to their kitchen windows then, as those windows had existed for more than twenty years, they would most likely have a claim to have the building removed. A strong but politely worded letter was therefore dispatched to the Haddocks pointing out these clauses, the unneighbourliness of their behaviour and the possible legal consequences which might follow if that behaviour continued. The letter also requested the removal of the new structure.

Letters of this style tend to have three possible reactions. Some recipients, afraid of lawyers and the law, would mend their ways immediately, thus bringing an end to the matter. Others took no notice and continued to behave exactly as they had before. A small but significant minority, outraged that anyone should have the cheek to dictate how they should behave in their own homes, viewed such letters as a declaration of war and intensified their anti-social behaviour accordingly. Mr Haddock fell firmly into the third category.

The Lemons were soon back in Frank's office, complaining of riotous parties most weekends, smaller but equally drunken affairs midweek and, most unacceptably in Mr Lemon's eyes, topless, and in Mr Haddock's case, completely nude, episodes in the hot tubs.

"He walks to and from the hot tub completely naked," he protested. "Then he stands, hands on hips, and stares at our house with a smug smile on his face, as if to say, 'What are you going to do about it?'

"My daughter Ellie's bedroom looks straight into his back garden – it's so embarrassing for her – and for Sheila. Isn't it, dear?"

Mrs Lemon nodded loyally.

"So we've agreed we are going to have to take this to court. We don't want to, but we feel we have no choice."

As always at this stage, Frank explained the high cost of litigation. He could not give a definite figure, as no one could tell at this stage whether the case would quickly settle or, at the other extreme, end up in a fully contested trial with evidence being given by witnesses and barristers instructed for both parties. Frank wondered if a round-the-table meeting might help to resolve matters, with both parties and their solicitors, or perhaps a more formal mediation process. But his client thought this would be a complete waste of time. Mr Haddock would not behave like a civilised human being unless he was ordered to by the court, and Sheila had recently inherited some money from her mother and they couldn't think of anything more worthwhile to spend it on.

So Frank took detailed statements from both of them, and over the next few days drafted the court claim and walked it down to the County Court for issue. The court would now list the case for a preliminary hearing and serve copies of the papers and notice of the hearing on the Haddocks. The Lemons, too, awaited the oncoming storm.

The expected storm failed to materialise though, with no furious pounding on the Lemons' front door by an indignant Mr Haddock waving the court summons. To his clients' relieved surprise, the behaviour from their neighbours was almost tolerable. And when Frank met his clients in the foyer of the court on the day of the hearing, they queried whether or not the Haddocks had been served. Frank installed them in a comfortable interview room and went off to ask the usher whether the defendants had turned up. It would make his life much easier if they hadn't.

He was to have no such luck. Outside Court 2, George, the circuit judge's usher, was in conversation with a short, squat, muscular man in his early forties, who could be none other than Mr Haddock. With him was an attractive, slightly embarrassed-looking woman several years his junior – Mrs Haddock, he presumed.

Frank introduced himself and asked the Haddocks if they were represented by a lawyer.

"We have a solicitor, but unlike our stuck-up neighbour, we've got better things to do with our money than waste it on you lot," was the predictable response.

"He's only asking, Ray," said Mrs Haddock. "Our solicitor has written to the court," she added, turning to Frank. "We've given the letter to the usher."

The letter explained that almost all the allegations in the court claim were denied except those relating to the Haddock's van. This they could hardly have denied, as Frank had obtained corroborating evidence in the form of a police report. It went on to ask the court to adjourn today's hearing to allow the Haddocks time to file their own evidence, and, bizarrely, on the facts as they were known to Frank, to file their own counterclaim. It suggested that the case then be relisted for a full trial with a time estimate of one day.

Frank's heart sank. This was not going to be the comparatively inexpensive victory by default which so many cases were. It looked like it would be a fight to the finish.

Frank explained the position to his clients to their growing disbelief.

"But, how can he deny everything; he knows it's all completely true. And won't it cost him just as much as it's going to cost us? Wouldn't it be cheaper and easier for him to simply behave like a civilised human being?"

"I think he believes that's what he is doing – his standards are different to yours. I've seen this in other similar disputes, they are the hardest cases of all to compromise. Unfortunately, it now means we ought to instruct a barrister for the second hearing. They are specialists in the presentation of cases in court – the cross-examining of witnesses. It will involve more expense, but if you win the court should order that the defendants pay a substantial proportion of your legal costs."

"Couldn't we oppose an adjournment?" asked Mrs Lemon. "And ask the court to deal with it today?"

"I don't think we would get very far with that. The court has five similar cases listed. It assumes that most will either not go ahead because, like ours, they're contested and need longer or because one of the parties doesn't turn up or they settle on the day. What we could try though is to ask the court to make an interim or temporary injunction not to park on your drive, as he seems to admit that."

Ten minutes later, the case was called and the parties were installed in Court 2 awaiting the arrival of the judge. The usher called for the court to rise and an elderly, bewigged gentleman, now becoming increasingly familiar to Frank, entered from the back of the court, took up his position before the imposing judicial chair and bowed to the assembled parties. Frank and his clients, taking their cue from Frank, bowed back.

Frank had last encountered Judge Peterson in the case of the Werewolf of Mannamead; on the face of it, he was a wise, genial old gent, but one who did not take kindly to bullies. Frank felt he might be the right judge for the case.

Frank introduced himself, his clients and also Mr and Mrs Haddock. Mr Haddock immediately interrupted.

"We are quite capable of introducing ourselves, thanks. Don't think you can take advantage just because we ain't got a solicitor."

"Mr Gilbert is just doing his job, Mr Haddock," the judge replied in his most reassuring tone. "It's the role of the plaintiffs' advocate to introduce the parties and explain to the court what the case is about."

Which Frank then did, as briefly as possible.

"Thank you, Mr Gilbert," the judge responded. "Now, Mr and Mrs Haddock, I have seen the letter from your solicitor – have you seen it, Mr Gilbert?"

"I have, Your Honour."

"And I understand, Mr and Mrs Haddock, that you want me to adjourn the case today so that you can prepare for a full trial of the issues. Is that correct?"

"Well, if they are really going ahead with this ridiculous case then I suppose we'll have to."

"Whether it's a ridiculous case or not is for me to decide, Mr Haddock."

Mr Haddock looked as though he was about to dispute that point but then thought better of it.

The judge now turned to Mrs Haddock. Frank was beginning to develop some sympathy for her as she seemed to squirm with embarrassment every time her husband opened his mouth.

"And what about you, Mrs Haddock? Do you agree with what your husband has said?"

"She does," her husband interjected.

"I am asking your wife, Mr Haddock, not you."

"Well, yes, I suppose we have no choice, though it's a shame we can't come to some amicable agreement with our neighbours."

Her husband shot her a disapproving glance and appeared about to take issue with her.

"That would certainly be the more sensible course, but I'm not sure your husband would agree with you. Do you think some sort of mediation might help here, Mr Haddock?"

"I'm not having some third-party busy-body telling me how to behave in my own home," he snapped back, still appearing to fume at his wife's disloyalty.

"Well, you might have to accept me doing that if the case goes to a contested hearing," the judge replied pleasantly. "So, Mr Gilbert, what do you say about an adjournment?"

"I suppose it's inevitable. But would you consider, Your Honour, granting an interim injunction on the issue of the parking in the shared drive? Mr and Mrs Lemon have set out in their witness statements how their lives have been made a misery by the defendants' behaviour – or should I say that of the first defendant – and if we could at least resolve that issue, so that Mr Haddock does not continue to block the shared drive with his builder's van, then life might be a little more tolerable for them pending the full hearing."

"Very well, what do you say to that, Mr Haddock?"

"I'm not agreeing to anything except an adjournment."

"In that case, Your Honour, perhaps I could ask Mr Haddock a few questions on oath about the parking issue?" Frank suggested.

"Very well, Mr Gilbert. Mr Haddock, would you mind going into the witness box for a few minutes so that Mr Gilbert can ask you a few questions?"

Mr Haddock seemed quite taken with the idea and was quickly sworn in. He enjoyed an audience.

Frank felt that the subtle approach would get him nowhere and piled straight in.

"Mr Haddock, do you accept you have trespassed on land owned by Mr and Mrs Lemon by parking your vehicle partly on their drive?"

"No, I parked it on mine."

Frank had not expected this.

"Have you read your solicitor's letter to the court?"

"Of course I 'ave."

"Can I read you the second paragraph?"

"You can do what you like."

"'My clients deny all the allegations in the plaintiff's claim,'" Frank read, "'except for that concerning the partial blocking of the drive. Mr Haddock accepts that his commercial vehicle is too large to fit entirely on his half of the drive and will not park it there again.' That's clear enough, isn't it?"

"Well, perhaps a few inches, but he could still get through."

"But when he tried to park on his side beside your van, you threatened him and he had to call the police."

"Yeah, and what a waste of police time that was."

"And do you accept that the police then asked you to move your vehicle?"

"No, they said it was a civil matter."

"We will be producing a copy of the police report at the adjourned hearing which will confirm they asked you to move."

"Well, if they did, I didn't hear 'em. Your client is a busy-body – nothing better to do than irritate his neighbours."

"But in Mr Lemon's statement, he says that your continuous antisocial behaviour, including your inconsiderate parking and constant partying, is making his life a misery. Do you—"

Mr Haddock interrupted.

"If their lives are a misery that's nothing to do with me; they should get a life and live a bit."

Frank had the distinct impression of rising judicial impatience throughout the cross-examination.

"Mr Haddock, please try not to insult the other party, otherwise you run the risk of giving me the impression that you are indeed a very difficult man to have as a neighbour," the judge said. "All Mr Gilbert is asking me to do is to order that until the main hearing in a few weeks' time you should not do something which it would be contrary to civil law for you to do anyway – that is, park part of your vehicle on your neighbours' land."

Frank wondered if he would be pushing things if he tried to expand the terms of the interim injunction a little.

"Your Honour, may I ask a couple of further questions?"

"If you must, Mr Gilbert."

"Mr Haddock, do you admit that you are accustomed to walking around naked in your back garden?"

"No."

"My client has photos."

"Lucky him, or do you mean her? Has Mrs Lemon been photographing me naked in the back garden?"

"Mr Haddock, you are trying my patience," the judge murmured wearily.

"Well, is there any law that says I can't be naked in my back garden?"

"There is if you are intending to offend your neighbours, and your neighbours are actually offended – you will see from their statements that they were," said Frank, taking over. "Your Honour, if you are willing to grant an interim injunction on the parking issue, would you also consider requiring Mr Haddock to wear trunks, at the very least, whilst in his garden?"

The judge pondered briefly.

"I will, Mr Gilbert, but I would appreciate some draft wording for that as it's not an order I've made before."

So the hearing was adjourned for a full trial in three weeks' time and the judge granted the injunction as Frank had asked.

As Frank explained the order to his clients in the foyer, Mr Haddock approached them. Frank anticipated a furious rant.

"Well, that was a hoot," he beamed. "I haven't enjoyed myself so much with my clothes on for a long time. I wish I had said I was a naturist and claimed the order breached my human rights – perhaps I'll save that one for the next hearing."

He didn't wait for a reply, but as they departed Frank noticed again that Mrs Haddock looked stricken with embarrassment.

"Strange man," said Frank, once they were out of earshot. "I feel quite sorry for his wife though. She doesn't look like she's enjoying this one bit."

He explained that he ought now to instruct a barrister to represent them at the full hearing and also a surveyor who would draw up a plan showing how the new building obstructed the light to their kitchen. Finally, he arranged a visit to their house in a couple of weeks' time to view the shared drive and the offending building for himself.

When he got back to the office, two letters sent in by Alec were awaiting him in what was becoming known amongst his colleagues as the Case of the Postman's Testicle. The first was from the Post Office, informing Alec and Drusilla that, with immediate effect and until further notice, no post would be delivered to their home address unless they made available a secure post box at the entrance to their land. Until then, their post could be collected from the Plymouth Sorting Office.

The second letter was from a firm of specialist personal-injury lawyers retained by the Post Office Union on behalf of the postman. It notified Alec and Drusilla that a claim for damages would be brought against them for personal injuries, including pain, suffering, loss of amenities and loss of earnings incurred by their client as a result of their failure to keep their dangerous dog under proper control. A medical report was being obtained and would be disclosed in due course.

After his earlier discussion with Alec, Frank had undertaken some research into the law regarding liability for dangerous dogs, looking in particular at the Animals Act of 1971 which he vaguely remembered from his course on torts at law school. Animals were divided into two categories: those that were naturally fierce, or *ferae naturae* in Latin, where a single act of aggression could be sufficient to impose liability on its keeper, and those considered naturally tame, or *mansuetae naturae*, for whose aggression a keeper would not normally be liable unless the animal had "previous". The expression "every dog has its day" therefore had some basis in law.

This seemed to Frank an eminently sensible piece of law. What seemed slightly less sensible, and to Frank somewhat surprising, was that a Rhodesian Ridgeback, a dog bred to hunt lions – and lions unsurprisingly were *ferae naturae* – and with such ample capacity to inflict injury, was considered naturally tame. Alec's postman would undoubtedly be very surprised to hear that. So as long as Potentilla had not previously transgressed, Alec and Drusilla might be off the hook – at least as far as the criminal law was concerned.

A quick call to Alec confirmed that this was indeed Potentilla's first act of aggression against a human. It was still possible though that there could be a civil claim. They would meet in the Minster in a couple of days' time to discuss matters further.

Later that week, Frank was installed in his usual corner of the Minster bar with his work colleague Dick Guildford-Brown, when Alec, characteristically late, finally rolled up for their meeting. As Frank had anticipated, Dick found the two cases currently occupying much of Frank's time highly amusing.

"Listen, Alec, old chum," he proposed. "We can kill two birds with one stone here. We need the loan of your bollock-biting hound so that we can let it loose in the garden of Frank's clients' naturist noisy neighbour. That should encourage him to keep his clothes on."

One of Alec's finer points was that he never objected to others having a laugh at his expense.

"Well, I'm glad I'm keeping the local legal profession entertained. But seriously now, things may be a little worse than I had imagined."

"Worse?" exclaimed Dick. "How can they possibly be worse than a large slavering hound biting the local postman on the bollocks?"

"Ha, ha, yes, I take your point but you know I told you, Frank, that she'd never done it before? Well, that wasn't quite true. Drusilla tells me that a few years ago, before we were together, she employed a local farm hand."

"OK, I can see where this is going."

"And she – Potentilla, that is – bit him quite badly on the buttocks."

Dick guffawed gleefully.

"What is it with your dog? She seems to have a fixation for the private parts of the human male."

"Did that get reported?" asked Frank, trying to restore a semblance of professionalism.

"No, it didn't. He wouldn't come back to work afterwards and Drusilla gave him six months' wages in compensation. Word might have got around locally though."

"OK, well, let's wait to see how your insurers respond – they might want to handle it in-house, or use their own solicitor. But if not then I'll need to meet with Drusilla to take a statement."

The following week Frank drew up outside the Lemons' house in his VW Golf. His modest vehicle fitted comfortably onto his clients' side of the drive. Mr Lemon was waiting for him in the garden.

"How have things been since we last spoke?" Frank asked.

"No better – worse if anything. He has taken to sitting in his hot tub, playing heavy metal on his ghetto blaster for hours on end. He was doing it just now but he must have known you were coming, as a moment ago it all went quiet."

He followed his client into the house where Mrs Lemon greeted him.

"The best view is from the upstairs back bedroom," she said.

He followed his clients up the stairs. They stood aside so that Frank could enter the small, quaintly decorated bedroom.

Out of the left window, Frank looked straight at a large timber-clad structure with a small chimney built against the boundary, about ten metres from his clients' house. It looked as if part of the building contained a sauna. It cast an obvious shadow over the whole of the back of the house.

Frank peered at the hot tub, the top of which could be seen in front of the wooden building. The larger of the two was the size of a small above-ground swimming pool.

"There's something floating in the hot tub – it looks like a backpack, and something else," said Frank.

Mr Lemon appeared alongside him and looked out.

"It's khaki- and flesh-coloured – my God, it looks like a body."

Frank looked harder.

"There's someone floating face-down in the tub!"

He pushed past his clients and sprinted down the stairs. There seemed to be no side route to the rear of the Haddocks' house, so he hammered loudly on the front door, which was quickly opened by an alarmed Mrs Haddock. His clients had now joined him.

"Quick, let me through – it looks like there's a body in your hot tub!"

The thought flashed through his mind that he would look a total idiot if this was a false alarm, and a backpack or toy boat or some other unmentionable inflatable object was floating in the tub.

He flew through the back door. The structure that confronted him was immense, with steps up to the decking platform which accessed both tubs. He noticed an electric lead stretched across the decking leading into the larger one.

"Careful, Mr Gilbert, water and electricity are not a good combination, we must switch it off," said Mr Lemon. "Where's the power point?"

A long extension cable led into the wooden building; Mr Lemon followed it in and Frank heard a click and at the same time an angry buzzing sound, which he had not previously noticed, ceased abruptly.

He turned and looked into the larger tub. Floating face down on the surface was the body of a large man. He knelt on the decking, leant into the tub and lifted the man's head. It was Mr Haddock, and Frank could tell immediately that he was too late. At the end of the electric cable, floating below the surface of the water, was the ghetto blaster. It would never blast again.

Frank now noticed Mrs Haddock staring up from the bottom of the steps with a lost, desperate look.

"I'm so sorry, Mrs Haddock, your husband's been electrocuted."

An ambulance was called, for what good it would do, and the police arrived shortly after – the same officer who had called previously but this time in the company of a detective sergeant. They would need to interview all connected parties, they said, including Frank, but they seemed to accept that the death had no sinister implications and soon left.

Frank was concerned for Mrs Haddock, whose reaction seemed one of bemusement. She wandered around the kitchen, moving items around and doing the odd bit of washing. He felt they couldn't just leave her alone in the house to await the undertakers. But consoling recently bereaved women was beyond his competence.

Mrs Lemon fortunately took control and put an arm around her neighbour's shoulder.

"Come on, dear, the housework will wait. Let me make you a nice cup of tea."

Five minutes later, all four of them were settled comfortably in the living room, sipping tea. Mrs Haddock plainly wanted to talk.

"Ray was such an idiot. I told him not to balance that radio on the edge of the tub. He always knew best, of course – as you know. He insisted on fitting it himself though he wasn't an electrician 'How could it fall in?' he said. Well, it did, didn't it?"

"Water and electricity don't go together," repeated Mr Lemon gently for want of anything more helpful to say.

"And, I'm sorry for all the trouble we've caused you. He was so stubborn – he had fallen out with the neighbours in both our previous properties, and one of those took us to court too. He could never accept that he was wrong about anything."

Frank was pleased that his clients had sufficient tact not to point out that all their problems were now solved – in any case they didn't need to.

"But now perhaps we can be friends; it was Ray who liked partying, not me. I'm Shelly by the way."

"Yes, we would very much like that, wouldn't we, Colin? And I'm Sheila."

Frank looked again closely at the widow, still intrigued by her reaction. She had shed a few tears, but could he detect beneath her subdued demeanour something approaching a sense of relief? Relief at the prospect of freedom from long years in the company of an overbearing, insensitive husband?

Perhaps – who could tell?

"Mrs Haddock, Shelly," he asked. "Do you have someone who could come and stay with you?"

"I'll ring my sister – she lives in Ermebridge. She'll pop over. She never got on with Ray though."

"And, until then, we'll look after you, dear," said Mrs Lemon kindly. "Don't you worry, Mr Gilbert, there's no need for you to stay, I know you're a busy man."

If Mrs Haddock's reaction to her husband's death was hard to read, the relief felt by his clients was plain as a pikestaff.

Frank hoped that when he finally kicked the bucket, the predominant emotion felt by those he left behind would not be relief.

Mrs Haddock and Mrs Lemon became great friends – or was it more a mother-and-daughter relationship? The court proceedings were withdrawn and his clients agreed to make no claim for costs against their new friend. They even allowed her to retain the sauna and changing room in place and became regular users of the new facilities.

Frank was never interviewed by the police and neither were Mr and Mrs Lemon. Had the police dismissed the affair too quickly? A mains-connected ghetto blaster balanced on the edge of a hot tub would need little coaxing to topple in – a little tap from a passing toe would do it.

Frank doubted that foul play was involved, but who could know for certain?

The Case of the Postman's Testicle generated some further correspondence, but then, as many cases do, seemed to peter out. A medical report was produced, showing that the testicle itself had only suffered bruising. The postman's manhood was intact and his prospects of fatherhood unaffected. The blood had come from a wound to the thigh.

Frank asked Alec about it a few weeks later. Was he to take witness statements or were the insurers' lawyers handling it?

"No need for either," was the breezy reply. "The case is settled."

"Settled? How?"

"The postman turned out to be quite a nice fellow and a great dog lover. He certainly didn't want Potentilla put down. It turned out he has a fascination for Ridgebacks, which is why he was climbing into the pen – he agreed he had been stupid. And it turns out that Drusilla teaches his wife – she is a student at one of Drusilla's evening classes."

"Did she take the opportunity to apologise?"

"No, none of that, you know what Drusilla's like. But what she did find out is that the postman and his missus live in a remote cottage on the moor. His wife is extremely nervous there – scared of intruders – and they have been trying to find a guard dog. So, quick as a flash, Drusilla asked her if she had considered Ridgebacks. The reply was that they would love one, but they were too expensive – Ridgebacks cost a fortune, four figures easily.

"'Well, how about two then?' Drusilla had suggested. 'On us – two bitches – only puppies at the moment but they'll grow up in no time. The females make better guard dogs – the female of the species and all that.'

"'What, you mean, you'll give them to us?' the postman replied.

"'Certainly, if you drop all this nonsense about damages.'

"Two days later, the postie was on the phone to accept our kind offer and to say that his solicitors would write to confirm the settlement in a few days' time, which they did."

"So, we're taking two of the puppies round to them in a couple of weeks when they're weaned. The Case of the Postman's Testicle is settled."

"Excellent," said Frank, "and did you sell the settlement to them by pointing out that the puppies had first-hand training from their mother in how to repel intruders?"

"Ha, ha," said Alec. "I didn't, but I will."